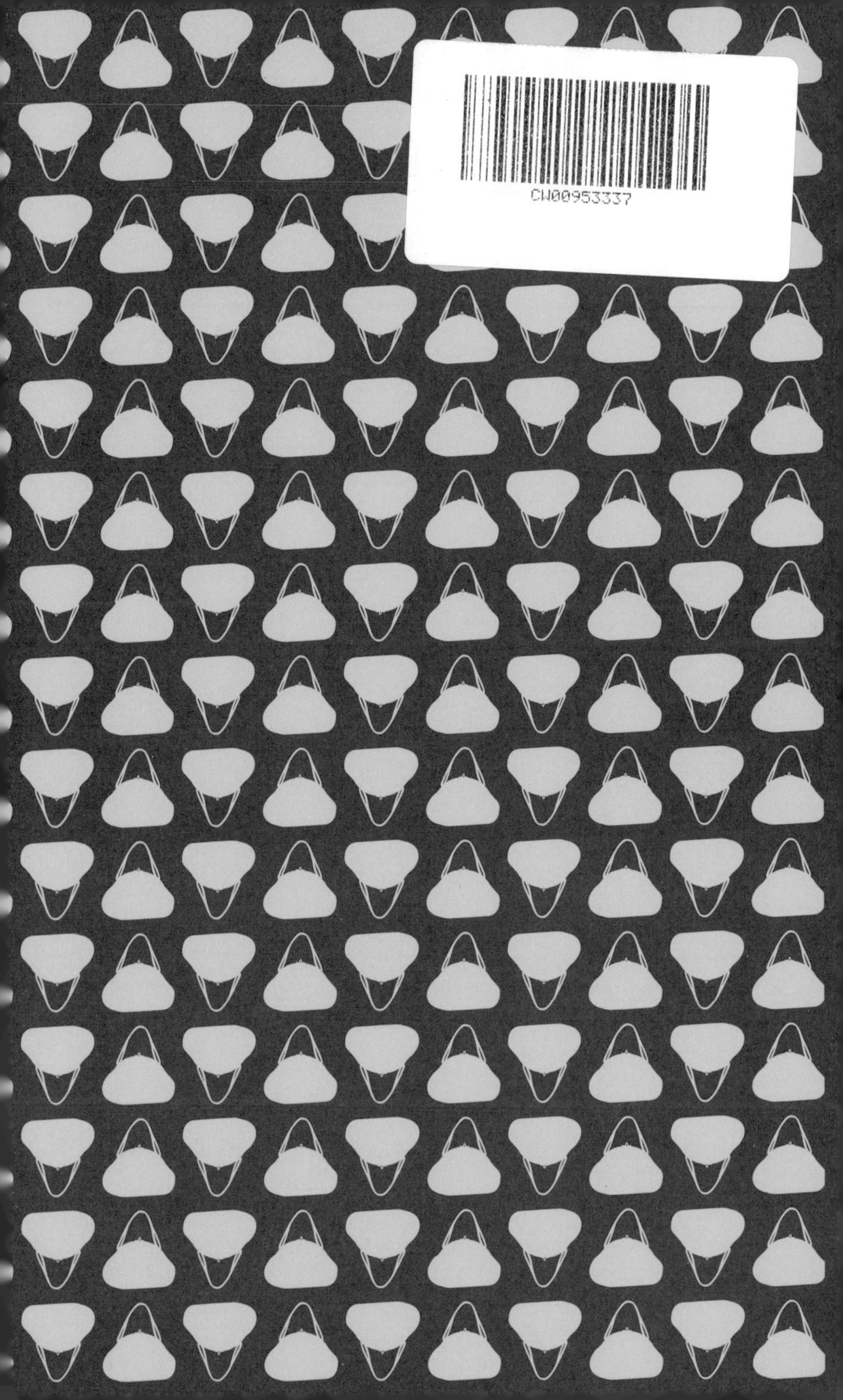
CW00953337

PRAISE FOR TONY BIRCH

'Birch evokes place and time with small details dropped in unceremoniously, and the stories are rife with social commentary.'

–*Weekend Australian*

'His metier is those who are economically and socially marginalised, and his deep emotional honesty when telling their stories resonates throughout.'

–*The Sydney Morning Herald*

'Birch's clear eye for detail, as well as for darkness and quirk of character, shines through at every turn.'

–*Books+Publishing*

'A sophisticated writer ... he nonetheless reserves the right to deal in his chosen subject matter with a simplicity and intermittent grace that has no ideological grounds beyond the desire to allow a story to tell itself.'

–*The Australian*

'Birch brings a softness to real and fictional spaces that is sorely needed right now.'

–*Readings*

Also by Tony Birch

Shadowboxing
Father's Day
Blood
The Promise
Ghost River
Broken Teeth
Common People
The White Girl
Whisper Songs
Dark as Last Night

WOMEN

CHILDREN

TONY BIRCH

UQP

First published 2023 by University of Queensland Press
PO Box 6042, St Lucia, Queensland 4067 Australia
Reprinted 2024

University of Queensland Press (UQP) acknowledges the Traditional Owners and their custodianship of the lands on which UQP operates. We pay our respects to their Ancestors and their descendants, who continue cultural and spiritual connections to Country. We recognise their valuable contributions to Australian and global society.

uqp.com.au
reception@uqp.com.au

Cover design by Jenna Lee
Cover photograph by Dawn Corcoran
Author photograph by Savanna Kruger
Typeset in 12/16 pt Bembo Std by Post Pre-press Group, Brisbane
Printed in China by 1010 Printing International

University of Queensland Press is assisted by the Australian Government through the Australia Council, its arts funding and advisory body.

A catalogue record for this book is available from the National Library of Australia.

ISBN 978 0 7022 6627 0 (hbk)
ISBN 978 0 7022 6813 7 (epdf)
ISBN 978 0 7022 6814 4 (epub)

University of Queensland Press uses papers that are natural, renewable and recyclable products made from wood grown in well-managed forests and other controlled sources. The logging and manufacturing processes conform to the environmental regulations of the country of origin.

For my mother – we made it out alive –
and for Debbie, Tracey, Kerrie, Sara, Renee, Raquel,
Erin, Siobhan, Grace, Nina and Isabel

'The body is the material expression of the
violence of the social world'
– Edouard Louis

ONE

THE NUNS WHO RAN OUR Lady's School shared the same first name. Mary. The head of school was Sister Mary Josephine, followed by her deputy, Sister Mary Agnes. Next in line was the head of junior school, Sister Mary Bernadette. And on it went. At the commencement of each school year the nuns paraded into the school hall, each wearing a starched white habit with a set of black rosary beads and silver crucifix drawn around the waist. With the arrival of the colder months of the year, the starkness was discarded for a dull brown colour, more appropriate for a school existing perpetually in the shadows of the church of the same name next door.

The church and school had been built in the late nineteenth century, indestructibly, from slabs of bluestone rock. Our Lady's Church sat in the middle of an inner-city suburb with a reputation for hard men and their crimes, from robbery and menace on the street to family violence behind closed doors. It was also a suburb of sectarian boundaries, with the Catholic community in no doubt that they lived under siege by Protestant leaders who dominated local government and business. Police were more likely to be Catholic, which produced mutually beneficial relationships between local crime bosses and the constabulary. Religious dedication was largely an affair of women and children. Most men never bothered with a conversation with God, leaving it to their families to attend mass and pray on their behalf for their numerous sins, at least until the men aged and became more concerned about the afterlife awaiting them. It was only then that they attempted a peaceful exchange with God.

The doors to the church had been shaped from lengths of heavy timber and were secured with brass hinges and locks. The building resembled a jail more than a house of worship, accurate to the point that the state's prison, north of the city, had been built from similar bluestone tablets. The stained-glass windows in the church were long and narrow and let little light into the building. The school itself looked as foreboding and drove fear into the hearts of children before they'd entered the schoolyard. Each classroom had a raised platform and blackboard at the front of the room, where the collective Sister Marys paced in a military fashion, keeping a watchful eye on their pupils, ready to pounce on any student who transgressed.

To the right of each blackboard sat an identical framed image of Jesus Christ. His hands were placed to an open heart and were cuffed in a reef of bloodied thorns. The image ensured that each generation of Our Lady's students were left in no doubt that Christ had not only suffered for their sins at the time of his death, but that He continued to bleed for them. In receiving the story of Christ's pain, children were taught that they owed a duty to God and his son. If they were to enjoy the glory of ascending to Heaven and avoiding the suffering of Christ, their single duty was to cleanse their bodies, both physically and spiritually, of sin. Consequently, Heaven was rarely spoken of by the nuns. Whereas Hell was an ever-present fear.

Sister Mary Josephine often reminded pupils what to expect were they to die with the stain of sin on their souls. At weekly assembly, each Monday morning, she demanded that students close their eyes and consider the extent of suffering they'd experience were they to place a hand into an open fire and leave it to burn for one minute. Sister would then ask that pupils imagine the intensity of pain were the heat of the fire increased one thousand times.

'Consider this,' she would call across the hall in a shrill voice, 'that not only has your hand been placed in the flames, but your entire body has become engulfed by the ferocity of the fire. Think of this and never forget it.'

She would calmly add that the suffering of Hell would never end. It would be experienced for an infinity – *forever.* 'You must imagine this,' she would announce, with many of the younger children in tears, 'that there will be no relief. Although you may beg for it to occur, your body will not be incinerated, and it will continue to burn. The experience of Hell will be far worse than anything you can imagine standing in this hall today. Therefore, you have an obligation to protect yourself against sin. As soon as you become aware that you have sinned, those of you who have taken the sacrament must immediately attend confession, beg forgiveness, and accept your penance with grace.'

The power of confession to redeem a person's soul was highlighted by a modern-day parable, a story of a criminal who had been miraculously saved from the fate of Hell. The tale often repeated was that of a notorious gangster who remarkably found his way to Heaven. It was a favourite story among students living on streets where crime competed with religion for ultimate authority. The gangster in question had been involved in crime throughout his life, including committing several murders, which, of course, were mortal sins. During a bank robbery the gangster was shot in the heart by police and lay bleeding to death in the gutter. A priest was called, the gangster confessed to his life of sin and last rites were administered. In that moment the slate was wiped clean, the gangster died, went straight to Heaven and was received by God.

Joe Cluny, a wide-eyed eleven-year-old boy in year six, listened to Sister Mary Josephine's sermons and stories of redemptive sinners with the conviction that he would struggle to get to Heaven unless a priest happened to be close by when he was near death. While trouble trailed some children at the school, it resided in Joe Cluny's back pocket. Although he never actively sought out mischief, Joe appeared unable to avoid finding himself on the wrong side of the nuns or the parish priest, Father Edmund, a severe man who ruled over his flock with a face so stern and frightening, he rendered students mute by his presence alone.

Joe had a dark birthmark covering his left cheek, which gave the appearance that he had forgotten to wash his face. Other children teased him over the birthmark, and he was quick to retaliate. The comments he received were sometimes playful but could also be cruel. During the holidays two summers earlier, his mother, Marion Cluny, had placed Joe with a local childminder, two streets away from their home. The woman was a chain-smoker with nicotine-stained teeth. She was also wafer-thin. Joe's older sister, Ruby, once said that the childminder reminded her of the raw chicken necks she'd seen in the front window of Garrett's butcher shop on the main street, an image that caused Joe to shiver with fear.

The morning that Marion left her son at the house the woman pointed at Joe's birthmark and told him that there had to be a *mongrel* in the family's past. 'Could have been an Abo. Or even a monkey,' she said, 'that come to your mother in the night and did her. Let's see if you have a tail.' She cackled and tried pulling Joe's pants down. He ran around the room until the childminder caught him and slapped his darkened cheek.

Joe touched his cheek and thought about the words of his late grandmother, Ada, who had once stood him in front of a mirror in her bathroom, placed the dark skin of an arm to his birthmark and said, 'That's the best of you, Joey. You and me both.'

The woman had several other children in her care, and she encouraged them to tease and mock Joe during the day. She also took his packed lunch away from him and fed it to her own children while he was ordered to stand in the corner of a room, face the wall and not speak a word.

At home that evening Joe told his mother what the woman had said and done. Marion was furious. Women in the suburb were never to touch another mother's child, let alone act with such cruelty. The following morning, Marion left Joe in the care of his grandfather, Charlie. She marched to the childminder's house and let her know that no local child would be left in her care again.

'You can't do that,' the woman said. 'I'm needed. Or these mums won't be able to work.'

'You're not needed that badly,' Marion told her. 'And you're the one out of work. For good.'

Marion let it be known among other women how Joe and other kids in the woman's care had been treated. By the end of the same week the childminder's business had ended and the front wall of her house was daubed with an insult: *Bitch*. She was spat at on the streets, and eventually moved away.

While Marion would not let another neighbourhood woman interfere with her children, discipline at school was left to the nuns and the priest. Joe's behaviour confounded his teachers, considering that his sister was one of the most accomplished students. Ruby was a grade ahead of her brother, in her first senior year. She had been awarded the prize of Dux of Class in each year from her commencement as a five-year-old and cast a long shadow over her brother.

At the end of each school day Ruby would sit at the kitchen table in the Cluny home and study, and she never went into the street to play with other children until her homework was completed. She also volunteered in the staff kitchen of a lunchtime, making cups of tea for the nuns and washing and drying dishes. While some of the nuns marked her for the convent after she'd finished her education, and the calling of a novice, Ruby's *choice* to become a model student had been an entirely calculated one. From her first weeks in school, she'd witnessed the humiliating punishment that children suffered at the hands of the nuns and set a path for herself to avoid a similar fate.

Marion Cluny was proud of her daughter's achievements. So much so that she'd papered one wall of the kitchen with the many certificates and prizes Ruby had been awarded over the years. During year six Ruby became the first and only student in the history of Our Lady's to correctly answer one hundred catechism questions across an arduous three-hour exam. A certificate that came with a prize had been framed and was the centrepiece of the kitchen wall display.

In addition to the certificate, Ruby was presented with a plaster statuette of Jesus Christ. It sat proudly on a shelf in the children's shared bedroom. At least until the afternoon Joe couldn't find a piece of chalk to draw a handball target on the wall of the factory directly across from the house. So he took the miniature Jesus down from the shelf and into the street, where he proceeded to use Jesus' head to draw the target.

When the statuette was returned to its place on the bookshelf later that day, Jesus Christ was missing his head, having been ground down to his shoulders. While Marion was furious with her son and banished him to the bedroom, Ruby remained calm, outwardly at least. She waited until later that night when Joe was in bed, almost asleep, before moving against him. Armed with headless Jesus, she jumped onto Joe's bed and pinned his shoulders to the mattress with her knees.

'Look what you did to my Jesus.'

Joe instinctively closed his eyes. When he was younger, he'd somehow convinced himself that when his eyes were shut and he was unable to see anyone around him, he also became invisible. Although he'd outgrown this most unlikely belief, the habit remained, particularly when he was confronted with danger.

'Open your eyes, you coward,' Ruby demanded. She shoved the statuette in Joe's face. 'You know you've had it? As far as sins go, Joe, this is as mortal as it gets. This is what Sister Mary Josephine would call *sacrilegious.* I might tell her what you've done, and she can give you the strap.'

Ruby dug the jagged end of Jesus into Joe's chest and slapped her free hand across his mouth to stop him from screaming to his mother to help him. She leaned forward and whispered in Joe's ear. 'There's no way back for you. Confession won't help you. Penance is a waste of time. Nothing can save you from Hell.'

While Ruby gained satisfaction from threatening her brother with religious punishment for his sins, she herself – unbeknown to her mother, younger brother or the nuns at school – was highly suspicious of Jesus, God the Father and religion generally. Her questioning of faith came at an early age for a child raised in the Catholic church. The moment Ruby suspected that she might no longer believe in God she understood it would be best to keep the thought to herself.

Her doubts surfaced after her closest friend at Our Lady's died. Back on her first day of primary school, Ruby sat next to a girl who had recently arrived from

Italy, Liliana Russo. Initially, Liliana couldn't speak English and the pair communicated through hand gestures and facial expressions, followed by a stumbling word here and there. By the end of their first year at school the girls had become inseparable. Each day they would share Liliana's lunch, a crusty roll filled with mortadella, cheese and pickle, while Ruby's tragically flattened Vegemite sandwich was thrown in the bin.

Around the middle of year four Liliana became sick, so ill that she would never return to school. When Ruby asked about her friend's absence from class, her teacher, Sister Mary Ruth, avoided the question. A month later Ruby and three other girls from her year were chosen to visit Liliana in hospital. Ruby would never overcome the fear she experienced walking along the hospital corridor. The walls were a dazzling white colour and the black-and-white chequerboard floor tiles appeared to shift as she walked across them.

She and the other girls were escorted into a ward lined with beds. On both sides of the room ill or bandaged children lay in a row. An isolation room, a glass cube, was at the far end of the ward, and the girls were not allowed to enter it. Ruby could see Liliana on the other side of the glass and silently mouthed 'hello' to her friend. Liliana lay under a white sheet and Ruby could hardly recognise her friend, who had become terribly thin and had lost most of her hair. The girl remained asleep throughout the visit.

Liliana passed away a week after the hospital visit. Her death was announced at morning assembly and her classmates were told to close their eyes and pray that her soul be cleansed of sin. Although Ruby obeyed and bowed her head, she felt angry and refused to pray. She couldn't accept that Liliana's soul would need saving from God or anyone else. She'd been a generous and kind girl, who couldn't have sinned in the eyes of Ruby. Walking home from school later that afternoon she decided, at nine years of age, that she would no longer pray to a God who had allowed her friend to suffer and die.

Joe had won no awards or certificates, except for ribbons for running races, a sport he excelled at. It wasn't clear to anyone, Joe included, why he was in trouble so often and spent more time than other students on the hard wooden bench outside Sister Mary Josephine's office. He was familiar with the full array of disciplinary punishments, including dragging a garbage bin around the yard of a lunchtime picking up rubbish, or the arduous task of emptying and washing several metal crates that were filled each day with empty milk bottles.

Each student was provided with a half pint of milk, to be consumed in the playground at morning recess. On warm mornings the milk heated before the children got to it. It was an offence, if not a sin, to leave any amount of milk in a bottle. Students were sometimes forced to drink warm milk, only to vomit it up soon after. Some children secretly emptied their half pint into the gully trap behind the nuns' kitchen, praying they wouldn't be caught. The bolder girls at school hid the bottles in their underwear, ran to the toilet block and flushed the contents down the bowl, enjoying a lengthy 'milk piss' as it was called.

The empty bottles, more than two hundred in total, were left in crates outside the tuckshop. Throughout the morning, dregs of milk fat congealed in the bottom of each bottle. To be thoroughly clean, the bottles had to be placed under a tap, rinsed and returned to the crate. When a milk ring had formed and crusted, a scrubber, resembling a miniature toilet brush, was needed to vigorously wash the inside of the bottle. The clean-up left the students' hands, hair and school uniforms reeking of rancid milk for the remainder of the day.

Two students, working together, would be occupied for the lunch hour to complete the task. A milk roster was attached to the noticeboard in the assembly hall on Monday mornings and all students above the two lower grades were supposed to rotate through the roster, although Sister Mary Josephine preferred using students who were serving time for bad behaviour.

Joe Cluny became an expert bottle washer during his years at Our Lady's and was often found at the gully trap of a lunchtime. On Ash Wednesday, during year six, he was cleaning milk bottles with a fifth-grade student, Daniel Faber. Both boys wore the mark of Christ, an ashen cross on their foreheads. Daniel's father was a local publican and the boy had been punished for bringing a bottle of beer to school in his bag. Daniel hadn't opened or drunk from it. All he'd done was show it to other boys in his class and remark that he could drink a bottle of beer anytime he wanted to. He just didn't want to at that time. He was caught when another student in his year, Rory Shannon, seeking to find favour with the nuns, reported Daniel to the class teacher, Sister Mary Bernadette.

As the boys scrubbed, Daniel explained to Joe the several ways he was going to kill Rory Shannon. 'I mean really kill him,' he said, shoving the brush into the neck of the bottle. While Daniel slaughtered a milk ring, Joe was watching an elderly woman standing on the other side of the school fence, on the footpath.

Although it was a warm day, the woman wore several layers of tatty clothing and a pair of knitted gloves pitted with holes. She supported one leg with a carved walking stick and repeatedly hummed to herself – the same tune, over and over.

The woman watched Joe closely as he tipped the remains of each bottle into the drain and washed them under the tap. He then handed them to the quality controller, Daniel, who inspected the bottles before placing them in the crate. The woman remained still, until the boys had completed the task for the day. She looked down at the crates of shining bottles and left, waddling along the street with her walking stick.

The following day, at lunchtime, the woman returned to the school, dressed in the same outfit. She carried a large metal bucket in one hand and her walking stick in the other. She stood beside the gully trap and began doing the work usually reserved for students. Rather than empty the small amounts of milk into the drain, she poured them into her bucket. She washed each bottle, just as she had seen Joe and Daniel do the previous day. By the time she'd finished, her bucket was almost full. When she left the schoolyard, the old woman struggled with the weight of the bucket.

She returned to the school the following day and repeated the task. Sister Mary Josephine stood in the middle of the yard and watched the woman for several minutes. Students whispered among themselves, expecting that at any moment the old woman would be ordered to leave. To their surprise, none of the nuns interfered with her and she again left with a full bucket of milk.

From that day forward the old woman came to clean the bottles and collect the leftovers. It wasn't known what she did with the milk, although some children, claiming that the woman was a witch, spread a story that she used the dregs to concoct a potion she then fed to stray cats across the neighbourhood, killing each cat with only a single lap of milk. Another story that circulated the schoolyard was that the woman had once been a nun, and she'd gone mad and left the order. Whichever story was attached to her, the woman was left alone to collect the milk.

With milk-roster duty no longer an option, punishment for even minor offences such as arriving at school wearing dirty shoes, or the vague offence of whistling in the corridor of a lunchtime, were confined to a range of cleaning duties around the school and in the church. More serious offences attracted corporal punishment, delivered with a black leather strap that each nun carried in a deep pocket sewn into her habit. No student, regardless of the seriousness of the crime, could be given more than six strikes. Some pupils broke down and cried before the whipping commenced, and few students could cope with more than one blistering strap on each palm without suffering excruciating pain. By the sixth stroke a student's palms would be bruised and sometimes bloodied.

Joe, who had been strapped many times, sometimes found himself in the contradictory position of praying to God to save him from a punishment about to be administered in the name of the same God. During his years at primary school his crimes were numerous. One would bring him lasting infamy.

TWO

ONE AFTERNOON DURING A YEAR six art class, Sister Mary Anne, a short and frail nun, the oldest sister in the school, stood on the platform in front of the class and instructed students to paint a face, either a self-portrait or the image of another student in the room. She then sat in a chair at her desk and was soon asleep. Joe stared at his blank sheet of paper for some time with no idea who he should draw. He glanced around the room. The faces of other students held no interest for him. Looking up at Sister Anne he was drawn to an object on her desk, a metal moneybox, the sculpted figure of a child who students mocked as *Black Sambo.* The moneybox was passed from one classroom to the next at the beginning of each week as a means of raising funds for the school's charity, with each class competing for the honour of collecting the highest amount of money.

One of the black child's hands was permanently outstretched and students were encouraged to come to class of a morning with a coin to drop in his palm. The moneybox child would then perform a trick. His mouth would drop open, his hand would snap back, and he would swallow the coin. Students enjoyed the performance and fed the black-faced child even more copper coins, chanting, 'Black Sambo! Black Sambo!' On Friday afternoons, just before final bell, Sister Mary Josephine would visit each classroom and announce the amount of money that had been raised in support of 'the poor coloured children of the missions'.

Joe felt sorry for the moneybox boy, being screamed at and passed from room to room for the entertainment of students. One morning, when Joe was in his second year, a group of boys had gathered around a desk where the moneybox boy was waiting to be fed. In unison, they beat their fists on the desk, yelling, 'Eat it! Eat It!' Joe looked directly at the moneybox boy and prayed that he could somehow find a way to fight back against the boys. The moneybox somehow managed to shift across the desk, fall off the edge and land on the tip of the ringleader's toe, fracturing it. From that day on Joe was in no doubt that the moneybox boy had powers that only he knew of, and that he and the boy were bonded to each other.

Joe sat at his desk and studied the boy's dark face for several minutes and decided to paint his portrait. Although not on paper. That afternoon, Joe would use his own face as a canvas. He dipped a brush into the black paint pot, lifted his fringe and daubed his forehead with paint. He then applied paint to his birthmarked cheek, until his lighter skin blended with the darker colour, and he no longer had a birthmark at all. Joe continued painting until his face was as black as the moneybox boy's own.

Seated next to him was a girl, Marlene Rizzi. She wore a bowl-cut hairstyle and had the rosiest cheeks, giving her the look of being permanently embarrassed. Joe was prone to talking in class and Sister Mary Anne had seated him next to Marlene, knowing that the girl would never speak to a boy in class, which managed to silence Joe for the day. He glanced across the desk at Marlene's sheet of art paper and wasn't surprised to see that she'd chosen to draw a picture of Jesus. Like most girls in the class and the nuns both, Marlene was deeply in love with Jesus and spoke about him constantly, as if Christ was a living person rather than a picture on a wall, a statue in the church or a headless figurine at home. Marlene was so deeply in love with Jesus she told other girls in class that when she grew up she would marry Jesus and present him with a virgin birth just as his mother, Mary, had done for Jesus' carpenter father, Joseph.

The golden hair and blue eyes of Marlene's drawing of Jesus closely matched the framed portrait of Christ next to the blackboard. Had there been a prize awarded for best portrait that day, Joe was sure Marlene Rizzi would have won. Sensing Joe's eyes on her drawing, Marlene turned towards him. Shocked by the sight of his black face, she screamed so loudly that Sister Mary Anne woke and jumped with fright from her seat. Joe, realising he was about to find himself in trouble yet again, ducked under his desk as the nun's chair crashed to the floor.

Craning her neck and searching the room for the offender, Sister Mary Anne spotted Joe's black face peering over the top of his desk. He looked oddly like a tortoise exiting its shell. Sister Mary Anne ordered Joe to the front of the classroom. Other students began to scream, some with fear, others with hilarity.

A boy seated in the front row, Martin Burke, called out to Joe and offered him a copper coin. 'Eat it, black boy.'

Marlene was asked to leave the class and bring Sister Mary Josephine from her office. The senior nun, on spotting Joe's painted face, pulled him by the back of his school jumper along the floor and out of the classroom. She dragged him down the hallway to her office and told him to sit on the wooden bench while she went to the staff kitchen.

'Do not move,' she said, pointing a hooked finger in his face.

Several students passed by Joe as he waited for the nun to return. Some laughed and others appeared disgusted. Joe smiled at each child and gently waved, content with the self-portrait he'd created.

A few minutes later Sister Mary Josephine returned with a bucket of ice-cold water in one hand and a towel in the other. The water sloshed around and spilled over the linoleum floor. Joe wondered what the purpose of the bucket was. Sister Mary Josephine sat it at his feet and commanded Joe to stick his head in it. He wasn't sure what she'd asked him to do. Perhaps he'd heard wrong.

'Put my head in the water?' he asked.

'Yes,' Sister snapped. 'And be sure to put your whole head in the bucket. Down on your knees. Now.'

Joe slowly knelt. Sister Mary Josephine clapped her hands together as if she was starting a footrace. Joe wished for nothing more at that moment than to be able to sprint away. Unfortunately, there was no chance of escape.

'Put your head in the bucket,' the nun repeated. 'Now.'

Joe plunged his head into the ice-cold water. The shock snatched his breath away. Sister Mary Josephine placed a hand on the back of his head and forced Joe's head deeper into the bucket. Gasping for air, he swallowed several mouthfuls of water. Looking into the bottom of the bucket, convinced he was about to drown, Joe tried to remember the last time he'd been to confession, anxious he might die with sin on his soul.

Sister Mary Josephine grabbed hold of the back of his neck and pulled Joe's head up. Hunched forward on his hands and knees, he coughed and spat mouthfuls of water onto the floor.

'Stand up,' the nun ordered. She handed him the towel. 'You wipe that dark filth from your face.' She watched closely as he cleaned himself.

Joe felt terrible pain on one side of his head, experiencing what he would later describe to Ruby as the most unimaginable ice-cream headache. 'Like two icy poles and a cream-between stuck in your mouth at the same time,' was the only way he could describe the sensation. He finished cleaning his face and handed the towel to the nun.

'You do realise what this means for you?' she said.

Due to a pounding headache, Joe wasn't sure what anything meant, except that he was likely to receive the strap in addition to the water torture. He looked down at the floor. 'I don't know, Sister.'

'Eyes to me,' she demanded.

He looked up. A wisp of silver hair protruded from the sister's habit. Some students at the school claimed that the nuns shaved their heads bald when they entered the order. Joe had never believed the story and felt a momentary sense of victory. He glanced from the sister's face to the set of rosary beads around her waist: Jesus was nailed to the cross, enduring even more suffering than Joe himself, and he had not painted his face at all.

The nun drew the leather strap from the pocket of her gown like a sword from a scabbard. 'I need you to put your hands out,' she said.

After being strapped three times on each hand, Joe was taken to see Father Edmund in the sacristy on the side of the church. His hands were burning and both palms were marked with bloodied welts.

Sister Mary Josephine bowed slightly towards the priest and spoke with him as if Joe wasn't present in the room.

'He has been a difficult child since commencing at the school. Nothing at all like his older sister, who has always been a diligent student. I do not know what to do with him. I believe he needs a firmer hand. Perhaps yours, Father?' *Another* strapping, Joe thought. 'He has no father of his own,' the nun added.

Father Edmund nodded his head. 'A home without a father's presence is nothing but an empty house.'

Although he should have known better than to do so, Joe couldn't hold his tongue and chose to correct the nun. 'I do have a father,' he insisted.

'Remain quiet,' Sister Mary Josephine demanded. 'The boy is also a liar, as you have just witnessed, Father.'

'But I have a dad,' Joe repeated, confused as to why the nun and priest doubted him.

Sister Mary Josephine, embarrassed that the priest might conclude she had no control over one of her more unruly students, grabbed Joe by the arms and furiously shook his body. 'You will stop this at once.' Sister was so angry, she involuntarily spat in Joe's face as she ordered, 'Be silent! Or I will have to give you another strap.'

Joe would like to have explained that another strap on the same day that he'd just received six cuts was illegal, as any nun and child in the school would know. He wisely chose to say nothing and stood quietly as the nun and priest discussed his predicament. Whatever amount of ill-discipline he'd been involved in, there would be no serious consideration of Joe, or any other

Our Lady's student, being expelled from the school. The diocese would not tolerate losing one of its children to the secular education system, which it regarded as nothing more than a front for Protestantism. Or, worse still, atheism.

Father Edmund decided that Joe would immediately attend confession and ask for forgiveness for the blackened face incident, in addition to his false claim of having a father. He would also be required to attend the church on the final day of term and complete whatever chores Mrs Westgarth, Father Edmund's housekeeper, instructed him to do.

After Sister Mary Josephine left the church, Joe went into the wooden confessional box. The air was stifling. It reeked of the priest's breath and body odour. Joe confessed to the lie he'd told about having a father, with the confession itself being a lie. He then asked for forgiveness for having painted his face black, which he wasn't sorry for at all. Because of his artwork he had brought the moneybox boy to life and frightened his classmates. He left the confessional with more sin on his soul than when he'd entered. For his penance Joe was required to recite six Hail Marys and three Our Fathers. A price he accepted.

That night, at the kitchen table, Joe hid his hands from his mother. Both palms were swollen and plum coloured. If she'd seen his wounds, Marion would have known that Joe had been in trouble again. His secrecy became threatened when Ruby announced to her mother, 'Joe had his head stuck in a bucket of water today.'

Fortunately for Joe, Marion didn't believe her daughter's story. 'Don't tease your brother like that. He gets in enough bother without you inventing stories about him.'

'I didn't make it up. The story is true,' Ruby said.

'Why would his head be put in a bucket of water?' Marion asked.

'Because Joe painted his face black.'

The story was now even less plausible to Marion. 'That's enough,' she said. 'You should know better, Ruby.'

At the end of the final day of term, Joe was tasked with cleaning the statues in the church. Mrs Westgarth provided him with both a damp and a dry cloth and a small step ladder to reach the taller statues of the Virgin Mary and another of Jesus Christ hanging from the cross. She took a packet of cough drops out of her pocket and offered one to Joe. 'These are the closest I have to a lolly. Would you like one?'

'Thank you,' Joe said. He took the cough drop out of the wrapper and placed it in his mouth.

'The word in the playground is that you painted your face black,' Mrs Westgarth said. 'Is that true?'

'Yep,' Joe said.

Mrs Westgarth laughed. 'You did that to yourself to disguise the dark mark on your cheek?' she asked, pointing at Joe's birthmark.

Joe hadn't thought so at the time but perhaps Mrs Westgarth was right. 'Maybe.'

'You were given a heavy sentence, in my opinion,' Mrs Westgarth said. 'A good lawyer might have got you off. It shouldn't be such a sin, painting your own face,' she added. 'I mean, it's all the go on the TV. *The Black and White Minstrel Show.* Me and my husband never miss it. Sunday night straight after the news. We love the show. You must have seen it? Maybe that's where you got the idea from.'

Joe never watched the minstrel show as it clashed with his own favourite, *Disneyland.* He had seen the opening number of the minstrel show one Sunday night when he was at his grandparents' house and his grandfather, Charlie, sat down to watch it. Ada, who was in the kitchen clearing the table, overheard the singing, came rushing into the loungeroom and switched the TV off. She turned to Charlie in a rage and said, 'Don't you ever watch this rubbish.'

'Is that where you got the idea?' Mrs Westgarth repeated.

No, Joe thought. Remembering his grandmother's anger, he wondered if she'd have been upset over him painting his face and now regretted what he'd done.

He looked around at the many statues he would have to clean. Several of them frightened him, never more so than during Lent, when they were draped with purple cloth and resembled ghosts. He began by dusting the Virgin Mary's head and outstretched arms. Joe had never realised previously, passing by her during mass each Sunday, that other than her head, arms and hands, the statue of Mary consisted of nothing more than a flowing gown. She had no legs or body. He knocked on the statue, around Mary's stomach, where she should be carrying the Baby Jesus. The Virgin was hollow inside.

When Joe had finished cleaning Mary, he moved on to Jesus, who wore only a loin cloth across his bloodied body. While climbing the ladder to reach his face, Joe studied the deep gash in Jesus' side, where He'd been speared. Many years earlier the wound had been painted a deep red by a priest, highlighting the attack on Jesus' body. Joe wiped Christ's hands, nailed to the wooden cross, then stood on the top step of the ladder and looked directly at Jesus, dusting the crown of thorns digging into his skull. He thought about pain and wondered if Jesus, who had suffered so much, would have been able to survive Sister Mary Josephine's fires of Hell.

Whatever lesson Joe may have learned dusting church statues, the experience did little to change his behaviour. In the second half of the school year Ruby concentrated on her homework each afternoon and Joe watched American television programs. Between the hours of four and six o'clock of an evening, until his mother arrived home from work, Joe dedicated himself to the box in the corner of the lounge that introduced him to fresh-faced children with perfect teeth, living in big white houses with front lawns and birds singing in leafy trees. During winter, with no heater in the kitchen, Ruby would do her homework in an armchair in the same room, in front of the gas heater.

The refrigerators inside the TV houses were as big as the Clunys' kitchen. When the children arrived home from school in the afternoons, they were met by well-dressed and coiffured mothers who looked as fresh as the children themselves, most likely because they had black women inside the big houses doing the housework for them, Joe believed. A child would open the refrigerator and snack on a roast chicken drumstick and cookies and milk. Joe watched each show as if they were documentaries rather than fanciful dreams. He ignored Ruby's complaint that television was nothing more than a make-believe world.

'None of what you see on the TV is true,' she complained to him. 'Nothing that you're watching every afternoon. None of those stuck-up kids wearing glasses. None of the quiz shows. Do you know they give people the answers to the questions before the show starts? And that the contestants have to give the prizes back after the show? Television is one big lie. Except for the news. Maybe.'

'You're the one making it up,' Joe countered.

'You believe that all this is real?' Ruby said, pointing to the television screen.

'I know it's true,' Joe replied. 'You're just jealous because you have to do homework instead of watching the tele.'

Ruby stood up. 'Watch this,' she said and turned the channel over to *Superman*, who at that moment happened to be leaping a tall building and was about to fly into the sky. 'You say TV is real? Let's see if you can do that.'

Each year a scheme was operated between the church and the school that allowed Catholic families from the countryside to offer holidays for children of the inner city. The program was designed for kids who had apparently never experienced fresh air or seen a cow or sheep, other than as a slab of meat on a baking tray going into an oven. Places were limited and Sister Mary Josephine had devised an elaborate points system for competing students, at each year level. Excellent grades in schoolwork drew premium points, alongside volunteering to hand out the donation plate at mass on Sunday or attend altar boy or choir practice. Poor behaviour and absenteeism from class or church resulted in demerit points, which provided offending students little opportunity to be chosen for a holiday. Marion Cluny had put her daughter's name forward at the beginning of the school year for the first time and it was expected that Ruby would win a place, being the most accomplished student in year seven.

A holiday was a rare experience for local children. During the long summer break, Joe and Ruby, along with other neighbourhood kids, spent their days at the nearby gardens catching yabbies in the duck pond and swimming in the free pool on warmer days. On Monday mornings during the summer months council workers filled the concrete pool in the gardens with fresh water. It was used by hundreds of children, and swimming more than a couple of strokes without bumping into another child was an impossibility. There were no toilets nearby, so *everybody* peed in the water.

By the end of the week the pool had turned a dull colour, somewhere between brown and green. It also had an odd smell that no-one could quite detect. Late on Sunday afternoons the pool was emptied, and the slime that had gathered around the concrete base was hosed down a rusting plughole in the centre of the pool. The walls were then scrubbed clean, all in good time for the pool to be refilled the following morning.

During an excursion to the swimming pool in the gardens Joe had once been taught a lesson by his sister. A family of children had sat nearby and stripped down to their bathers. Joe could see that each child carried both fresh bruises and old scars on their bodies. He leaned across to his sister, pointed in their direction and whispered, 'Look at those kids. They've been hurt.'

Ruby grabbed him by the arm. 'Don't point, Joe. And don't you ask,' she added. 'Never ask.'

He realised his sister was angry with him, but Joe had no idea why. 'I can't ask?' he said. 'Why not?'

'Because you never do, that's all,' she said. 'Not about bodies.'

Although what Ruby had said made little sense to

him at the time, Joe never forgot her words and didn't ask about the origins of any child's battle wounds again. Over time he would come to understand the importance of her words without realising how that had occurred. Like most of what he learned on the street, he somehow absorbed what he needed to know without having to be told more than once, if at all.

In the last week of school, many months since the black-face incident had happened, the finalists for the holiday program were announced at morning assembly. As the names were read aloud to the gathered students some children squealed and clapped, although a few dropped their heads, realising their chances of a holiday away diminished with each name that was read out. No-one present in the hall that morning, not a nun or student, was surprised when Ruby Cluny's name was announced to the assembly.

She broke the news to her mother over the tea table that night. Joe watched his mother's face for a reaction. Marion Cluny wasn't a woman to openly express emotion in front of her children and appeared neither excited nor disappointed on hearing the news. 'I'll need to buy you some new underwear for the trip,' was all she said to Ruby.

On the morning of the last day of school Joe was met by Mrs Westgarth at the school gate. She'd taken a shine to him and said that she had a surprise for him. 'Come by the church before you leave today,' she said. 'I've something for you.'

Joe went to see Mrs Westgarth following the afternoon sports class and she presented him with a round tin. 'Open it,' she said. Inside was a cream sponge with whipped cream and fresh strawberries on top. Joe's mouth watered.

'Do you like it?' Mrs Westgarth asked.

'It's so beautiful,' Joe said. 'Thank you.'

Mrs Westgarth kissed his stained cheek and wished him a merry Christmas. 'You take it straight home before the cream melts.'

Delicately carrying the cake tin, Joe went back to his classroom to collect his schoolbag from his desk. The room was empty. He slung the bag over his shoulder and balanced the tin in his hands. About to leave the room, he noticed that the moneybox boy sitting on the nun's desk was watching him, in the same way that he'd looked back at Joe on the day he'd fallen from the table and broken the toe of the boy teasing him. Joe walked onto the platform and looked closely at the boy. 'Will you be lonely over the holidays?' he asked.

He put his bag on the floor and the cake tin on the nun's desk. He turned the moneybox boy around, released the metal catch on the back and opened the money drawer. After tipping the copper and silver coins onto the desk, he closed the drawer. 'You can come home with me for Christmas,' he said, and placed the moneybox boy in the bottom of his schoolbag.

When he arrived home, Joe hid the moneybox boy in his wardrobe, behind his football boots. That evening, the family enjoyed Mrs Westgarth's gift of cake with a cup of tea.

'You must have done something good to earn this,' Marion said to Joe. 'Well done.'

'I don't think so,' Ruby offered, biting into a slice of cake. 'Mrs Westgarth feels sorry for Joe because he's always in trouble.'

The following day a letter was posted home from the parish office. It contained the instructions for Ruby's holiday. She would be staying with a family across the state border, on a farm. The letter explained that the sponsoring parents had four children of their own.

'Why do they need Ruby then?' Joe asked his mother. 'If they already have kids of their own, they don't need another one. I wouldn't go if I were you,' he suggested to Ruby. 'You'll probably have to work on that farm. Like the slaves used to.'

'But you're not me,' Ruby snapped. 'And you're going no place, Joe, because you can't stay out of trouble at school. So, shut up.'

Their mother interjected in the argument. 'Don't ever tell your brother to shut up, Ruby. You tell him to be quiet.'

'Be quiet.' Ruby smirked.

Ruby would be allowed to take one small case with her, containing two spare sets of clothing and underwear, as well as a second pair of shoes and a packed toilet bag. The instructions with the letter also explained that she could also take a maximum two books and a skipping rope, even though Ruby had never skipped a rope and wasn't about to. She would need to be on time at Spencer Street railway station early in the morning, where she would catch the train that travelled north for five hours. Ruby would be met by a priest and the host family at the other end of the line.

On the morning she was leaving, Ruby woke early, washed and ate breakfast while her mother made and packed a lunch of ham and pickle sandwiches on brown bread, two pieces of fruit and a bottle of lemon cordial.

Joe waited to say goodbye to his sister in the kitchen.

Ruby was sparkling clean and smelled of fresh soap. She wore a white cotton dress and her raven hair was tied in pigtails with red satin bows at the ends. She had an envelope pinned to her dress with her name and address written on the front. 'If you don't like it there, you can mail yourself home,' Joe joked.

Although he would never have said so to her face, Joe thought his sister looked beautiful. Before leaving Ruby kissed him on the opposite cheek to his birthmark, which she liked to refer to as his 'evil side'. Her kiss was a rare display of affection between the siblings. They then shrugged in tandem, as if it meant nothing to either of them that they were about to be separated for the first time in their lives.

It wasn't until that night when Joe was in bed that the reality of Ruby's absence struck him. He looked across at the empty bed on the other side of the room and buried his face in a pillow.

Later in the night, unable to sleep, Joe got out of his own bed and went across to Ruby's, which sat under a window. He pulled the curtain back and looked up at the sky. It was a clear night. Whenever he felt too anxious to sleep, when he thought he might die in the night and be sent to Hell, Ruby taught him to count stars, explaining that, at first, he'd only notice a few of them in the sky. But that once he'd learned to concentrate, he'd find more stars, until there were so many to count that he'd fall back to sleep.

Joe began counting and hoped that, at the same moment, Ruby might also be searching the same sky that he was and thinking of him.

THREE

Marion Cluny worked at a dry cleaners on the main street. She started behind the counter at the shop straight out of school, the year she turned sixteen. Church spires marked both the south and north boundaries of the street, the Catholic cathedral at one end, located on a hill overlooking the city, and a brooding Protestant outpost at the other. The shopping strip that the churches bookended was home to several busy hotels, nightclubs and gambling dens hidden behind curtained shop windows, run by Italian and Greek immigrants. Trams rattled along the street from early mornings until late at night, newspaper boys vocally plied their trade from every intersection, and women wheeled the footpaths on both sides of the street, with prams, shopping trolleys and fuel carts.

Marion was due back at work in the week after the new year's holiday. On the Sunday before her return she made lunch for herself and Joe and sat with him at the kitchen table. 'I'm back in the shop tomorrow,' she said.

Chewing a mouthful of bread Joe nodded his head with no more than mild interest. He was looking forward to his mother returning to work. He'd have the freedom to run the streets with his schoolfriends unsupervised. Unfortunately for Joe, his mother had other plans for him.

'I can't leave you on your own while I'm at work,' Marion said, having read Joe's thoughts. 'I've spoken with your grandfather, and he agrees with me that it's better if you spend weekdays with him. At least until Ruby's back home, when she can watch out for you until school starts back.'

'Char can't mind me,' Joe replied, in hope. 'He has to be at his sweeping job?'

'Have you forgotten already that your grandfather finished up? It was only two weeks ago.'

Joe had forgotten. His grandfather had worked as a streetsweeper on the local council for over thirty years and had retired a week before Christmas. On the day he left the job Charlie Cluny was presented with a wristwatch and a new street broom with his name engraved on the copper handle.

Joe loved his grandfather, who he'd called 'Char' from the day he'd first awkwardly mouthed his name. He liked to visit Char on weekends and search through the many items, stored in his shed, that had been collected from the streets over the years. He also enjoyed sitting at the kitchen table with Charlie, listening to the stories his grandfather told. But as much as he enjoyed his grandfather's company, Joe had not expected to spend entire days with Charlie over summer.

'Tomorrow boys from school are going to the gardens for a swim,' he said. 'Maybe I can go to the pool in the morning and then to Char's after lunch?'

'You could do that,' Marion said, 'but it's not happening. Tomorrow morning I want you up early. You'll dress and have breakfast with me, and I'll drop you to Charlie on my way to the shop.'

'Will I have to stay with him all day?' Joe asked, certain of the answer.

'You will. All day, every weekday, until Ruby is home.'

The three-roomed house and yard Charlie Cluny had lived in throughout his married life was organised in a manner that made sense to him, but possibly no other person. He'd swept the streets of the suburb for most of his working life and had become a dedicated collector of the goods that others discarded. One side of his backyard had been set aside for growing vegetables. Charlie's tomatoes were legendary. An open tin shed lined with shelves and wooden crates ran the length of the other side of the yard. The shed was a treasure-trove for anyone searching for an item they'd prefer not to part with money for. If Ruby or Joe or any other child from the neighbourhood lost a tennis ball, football, rounders ball or ball of any description, Charlie had an overflowing crate to choose a replacement from. He also had a shelf lined with dolls, some missing an arm or a leg, buckets of marbles, and ball bearings and pram wheels available to power a billycart. If anyone was after a saw, hammer or ladder, Charlie had one on hand, although some were rusted or broken, and in need of repair. He'd also collected oddments, some bordering on the bizarre. Charlie had a naked store mannequin guarding the backyard toilet, a stuffed rabbit in a glass case in the laundry, and two boxes of new woollen socks, samples apparently, with the toes cut out in a top drawer of the kitchen cabinet.

In recent years, he'd surrounded himself with books and record albums in the kitchen, although he no longer owned a record player. The one he'd previously owned had gradually lost speed, with forty-five records playing on thirty-three speed, and the thirty-three albums reduced to an agonising moan. Charlie had been waiting for a replacement to turn up on the street, but it was yet to arrive. Under the kitchen table sat a tea chest full of the photographs he'd found on a street corner one early morning. Portraits of anonymous people with no story to tell except for the occasional date and caption on the back: *Uncle Roddy – Christmas 1948.*

Charlie's late wife, Ada, had restricted his collectables to the backyard. Following her death, five years earlier, he allowed himself the indulgence of moving the book and record collection, as well as the photographs, into the kitchen. The books in particular provided Charlie with company, relief from bouts of depression brought on by the loneliness he experienced missing Ada. Although he hadn't made it beyond grade six at school, Charlie had become a dedicated reader after many years of struggle. When Ada couldn't find him anywhere around the house, she'd track Charlie to a battered leather armchair that sat in a corner of the open shed, where she would discover him reading, or at other times asleep with a book in his lap after a hard day's work on the broom.

The day after Ada's funeral, Charlie carried the

reading chair into the kitchen and sat it by the kitchen table. When he wasn't reading, he enjoyed reaching a hand into the lucky dip of photographs. He'd pull out a picture, study the people in the image, and become puzzled by the thought of what could motivate a person to throw away the memory of a mother nursing a newborn in her arms. Or another, of a family standing in front of the bird enclosure at the zoo, a father resting a hand on the shoulder of a child.

Joe walked along the side of the house, knocked, and waited for his grandfather's greeting of 'hello' before opening the door. Charlie was standing at the stove tending a sizzling pan. His hair and beard had turned prematurely snow-white years earlier. Charlie had never appreciated the shock of silver and complained that it made him look older than his years. Ada loved the colour and washed Charlie's hair each Sunday night, flattering her husband, telling him that his silver mane gave him a distinguished look: 'Even smarter looking than you actually are, Charlie.'

When Joe was a small boy, before he had started school, and could discover almost any toy he wanted in his grandfather's shed, he had convinced himself that Charlie was Father Christmas. Until Ruby crushed another of his fantasies, bluntly telling Joe that their grandfather could not possibly be Father Christmas, as no such person existed.

'He does exist,' Joe had protested. 'Father Christmas is a real person.'

'Have you seen him?' Ruby asked, mocking her brother.

'Yep. Father Christmas is Char,' Joe explained.

'He can't be both Father Christmas and our grandfather.'

'Yes, he can,' Joe countered. And around and around the argument continued.

Charlie turned to Joe and smiled. 'Have you had your breakfast?'

'I had toast with butter,' Joe said, smelling the frying bacon.

'That's not breakfast. Toast is only a warm-up. An *entrée*, fancy people call it. Sit at the table and I'll make us bacon sandwiches.'

Joe looked up at the shelf over the stove and noticed that Charlie had moved a new collection into the house since he'd last visited. Antique glass bottles of different shapes and colours.

'I bought the bottles in yesterday morning and

soaked them in the trough with bleach,' Charlie said, pleased that his observant grandson had spotted the addition to the kitchen. 'When the sun hit the window yesterday afternoon, it struck the bottles and the wall was splashed with colour. You'll see it later today. The blue colours are truly beautiful.'

Charlie stabbed the frying bacon with a fork, transferred the strips to thick slices of buttered bread and smothered the bacon in tomato sauce. He brought two plates to the table and sat down across from Joe. 'Now, this is a proper breakfast. I have salt and pepper if you want it.'

Joe picked up his sandwich and bit into it. The bacon burning his tongue didn't stop him eating.

'Do you like your sandwich?' his grandfather asked.

Joe waited until he'd stopped chewing. 'I love it.'

'I don't doubt it.' Charlie picked up a knife and cut his own sandwich into fours. 'When I was on the broom, I had a bacon sandwich every morning before work. Couldn't start the day without my sandwich.'

'Do you miss the broom?' Joe asked.

'Yeah, I do,' Charlie said. 'And the people on the street. I miss them. But not as much as you must be missing your sister, away on her holiday. Has she written to you yet?'

'Nup,' Joe said. 'When Ruby was leaving for the train,

she said she'd send a postcard. I check the letterbox every day. There's been nothing.'

'She'll be too busy to write, I'd expect.' Charlie held one of the four squares of bread between a callused finger and thumb. 'Maybe you'll get the chance to go away at the end of this school year?'

'If I can stay out of trouble.' Joe smiled across the table. He didn't seem concerned that his chance of a holiday away would most likely again be less than slim. Sitting in his grandfather's kitchen eating a sandwich would be plenty for him until he was able to enjoy a day at the free swimming pool with his friends.

'What trouble was it that you got into during the year that disqualified you from a holiday?' Charlie asked.

Joe looked up from his sandwich to Charlie's mischievous eyes. His grandfather was fishing for an answer and they both knew it. Joe could have lied but understood it would be a waste of time. He was certain that Charlie knew the answer to his own question. Joe's grandfather appeared to instinctively know what Joe had been doing with himself, particularly when it involved trouble. Joe believed that Charlie could most likely read his mind.

When Joe didn't answer, Charlie prodded the boy. 'What I heard, some time ago now,' he said, 'is that you painted your face black, to match the face of the boy on the moneybox in your classroom. Would I be right?'

Joe's mouth was stuffed with bacon and bread, and he couldn't speak. He nodded in agreement with his grandfather.

'You know that poor boy has been stuck in that classroom since I was younger than you?' Charlie said. 'He would be a millionaire this day had he been permitted to keep even half the coins he's swallowed over the years.'

Joe allowed himself the slightest smile, thinking that the moneybox boy was no longer stuck in the classroom at all but was resting comfortably at the bottom of his wardrobe. He glanced across the table for any sign that Charlie might suspect the theft.

Charlie picked up another square of his sandwich and studied it before placing it in his mouth, as lightly as a priest would rest a communion host on a parishioner's tongue.

'Tell me something, Joe. What was it that persuaded you to do such a thing? Paint your own face black?'

Charlie wasn't angry at his grandson. He was simply curious.

Joe wiped bacon grease from his mouth with the back of his hand. He didn't believe that it was a good idea to tell Charlie that the moneybox boy had magical powers. Or that he wanted to have the same colour skin, which he couldn't make sense of himself. 'Because I like him, and I thought it would be good for me to look the same as him.'

'There's the explanation for the trouble you found yourself in,' Charlie said, slapping his hands together. 'The Sisters, they can't have you liking the boy on the moneybox. He's their prized charity case and you're supposed to pity him and feel sorry for him. Not treat him like a friend. Or want to be like him. They couldn't cope with that.'

Joe chewed on a crust of bread, contemplating what his grandfather had said. 'How did you know?' he asked.

'How did I know what?'

'How did you know that I painted my face? And that I got into trouble from the Sisters? When Ruby told Mum what I'd done wrong, she didn't believe the story, and told Ruby to keep it to herself. Did she tell you?'

'Your sister told me nothing. I know because I always do,' Charlie said. 'Remember I worked every street in the suburb and that I know every corner, every gutter. I'm on a first name basis with each brick. I also know every face that matters. It's not hard for me to find out about trouble that my grandson has been up to.'

Joe slumped in his chair, dismayed that he would never be able to keep a secret from Charlie.

The old man's eyes twinkled like a child's, and he smiled cheekily. 'To be honest with you, Joe, Mrs Westgarth, the priest's housecleaner, she told me what you'd been up to.'

The incident had occurred months earlier. Joe wondered why his grandfather had kept his knowledge of the incident from him. 'When did Mrs Westgarth tell you?' he asked.

'Sometime late in the winter,' Charlie said. He leaned across the table. 'And I know what you're thinking right now,' he said. 'Why have I waited until this morning to talk to you about what went on back then? Would I be correct?'

'Yep,' Joe answered, now certain his grandfather was a magician.

'Well, I wasn't sure if your mother knew what had happened and I decided it would be best not to speak to you about what had gone on. Not in front of her, at least. This is our first catch-up alone for some time,' he added. 'I want you to know there is no need for you to ever keep a secret from me. I wasn't angry when I heard about you painting your face. There's a hundred ways to get on the wrong side of the nuns. They're as mad as cut snakes, every one of them, even the quiet ones. There's little they don't find fault in. You just happened to have committed an offence that hadn't been considered until recently. But from here on? It could become the eleventh commandment, I'd expect. *Thou must not paint thy face black.*' He tapped the side of his head with a finger. 'You must learn to box smart and stay out of harm's way, Joe.'

'Box smart?'

'Yeah. I'll teach you the technicalities some other time. For now, all you need to know is one of the basics. Think before you act is a good start. Would you still have painted your face if you'd given it proper thought?' Charlie asked.

Joe reckoned he'd given the idea plenty of thought and didn't consider that he'd act any differently. He looked over at his grandfather and grinned. Charlie had tomato sauce in his beard.

'What are you laughing at?' Charlie asked. Joe pointed to the beard. His grandfather wiped his face and ate the last square of his sandwich.

'Mrs Westgarth is of the opinion that you were treated poorly. She couldn't believe that you'd got the strap, was ordered to confession, and had to clean the church as well. How do you go handling the strap?'

Joe opened his right hand and showed it to Charlie.

A scar ran diagonally across his palm. It resembled a line of fading blue ink. 'I have this,' he said.

Charlie could hardly believe what he was looking at. 'You're still marked from the day you painted your face?'

'No. This one is from a couple of weeks ago. Just before school break-up. I got the strap, one on each hand, because I was talking to another boy at morning prayers.'

'You were strapped for talking?' Charlie couldn't contain his anger. 'A fucking disgrace,' he said, before apologising for swearing, a regular habit of his. 'You would have to be hit with some force to leave a mark like that on your hand. Has your mother seen this?'

'Nup,' Joe said. 'I haven't shown her. If Mum sees the scar, she'll know I've been in trouble again.'

'I know who should be in trouble,' Charlie said. 'The hags who run the church. Or Father Edmund, who has the reins on them. You need to show your hand to your mother, Joe. I thought the days of a whipping had ended.'

Charlie had attended the same school as his grandson over half a century earlier.

'When you were a boy, did you get the strap?' Joe asked.

'I certainly did,' Charlie said. 'I was always in strife.'

He lifted his chest, as if he was proud of having also been a troublesome boy in school.

'Let me give you a survival tip. I used to rub both hands on the arse of my school pants just before the strap was coming. Getting heat into your skin eases the pain.'

'Did you learn to behave?' Joe asked.

'Learned very little. I never liked school and got out as soon as I could. My mother, your great-grandmother, she was very unhappy when I told her I wanted to give it away. Soon as she realised she couldn't talk me out of it, she said she'd only tolerate me leaving if I walked out of the school gate and into paid work. And that's what I did. A few years in the boot trade and then I went onto the council street sweeping.'

Joe had always felt proud that his grandfather kept the streets clean and tidy for people in the neighbourhood. 'How old were you when you left school?'

'I was eleven. The same age as you are now.'

Charlie stood, gathered both their plates and read his grandson's thoughts yet again. 'And don't you get an idea into your head about following in my footsteps. Life is different now.'

'But I could sweep the streets like you did,' Joe said.

Charlie laughed at the thought. 'I have that new street broom they awarded me on retirement out in the backyard. You're welcome to try picking it up. It weighs more than a road shovel. Working with a broom all day takes muscles that you don't have, boy. Anyway, your mother will want something more for you than a life picking up rubbish after people.'

Joe looked over to Charlie's homemade bookcase, each shelf crammed with dog-eared paperbacks and magazines. 'None of this is rubbish. Maybe I could become a collector like you.'

'A collector. You could surely do that. It's most likely in your blood, seeing as collectors are born, not made. Whereas labourers are only ever made. By the bosses. But it's best to keep collecting as a hobby and not a job. That way you'll enjoy it more.'

'What job do you think I could do?' Joe asked. 'When I'm older.'

Charlie took the question seriously. 'Let me see. You love your reading, I know that. I think that you could grow up and become a writer.'

'A writer?' The suggestion surprised Joe. He'd no idea that being a writer could ever be a job.

'Yes. A writer,' Charlie repeated. 'There are stories about this life, the life of our family, that will one day need to be told.'

'Like the stories you tell me?' Joe asked.

Charlie paused. 'Maybe. But more than that. There

are stories that none of us are ready to tell. Some that we'd prefer to keep to ourselves. They're the same ones you'll have to write. People will need to know,' he added, with an odd look of concern on his face.

'Like secrets?' Joe asked.

Charlie smiled slightly but did not answer. He put the dishes in the sink, passed a tea towel to Joe and began washing up. 'Are you ready to work?' he asked. 'Now that I've retired, I have a big job ahead of me that I need help with.'

'What's the job?'

'I need to get the backyard in order. I have so many years of collecting out there that needs seeing to. Are you available to help?'

Joe felt honoured that his grandfather had requested his assistance. 'I am, Char.'

'Good. We'll need to discuss your pay rate, of course. We can negotiate at lunchtime if it's okay by you. Let's finish the dishes and get started out back.'

Charlie opened the rear of his car, a beaten-up station wagon, and walked across to the shed. A pile of twisted metal and copper piping lay on a sheet of canvas. 'First up, we need to take this lot to Ranji Khan's scrapyard. You load the copper pipes and I'll look after the lead.

It's the heavier metal. You know my mate Ranji?'

Joe knew about the scrapyard, as Charlie had talked about it often. But he'd never met his grandfather's friend, who was the owner. 'No. I don't know him.'

'Well, I'll introduce you to Ranji today. You two will get on fine with each other.'

Joe was keen to test his strength. He picked up a length of pipe, followed by a second and a third.

Charlie watched him closely. 'Take it easy. If you keep the heavy lifting up you'll put your back out of action before lunchtime.'

'Where did all of this stuff come from?' Joe asked, loading the scrap into the wagon.

'Wrecking sites, mostly. When a building is knocked down, this is what's left behind. Metal is the bones of a building. And the veins. This stuff carries the gas, electricity and water. It keeps a building alive.'

'And you collect the bones?' Joe asked.

'I do.'

'Is it stealing?' Joe said, picking up another length of pipe.

Charlie laughed out loud. 'Jesus, I hope not.' He looked around the shed, packed tight with the many years of stripping derelict buildings of scrap metal. 'If this is thieving, there'll be no way back from Hell for me.'

Once they'd finished loading the wagon, Charlie ordered a stop-work, went into the kitchen, and returned with two glasses of cordial and a packet of biscuits.

Joe was thinking about what his grandfather had just said. 'Are you afraid of Hell?' he asked.

'Whoa. That's a big question, Joe. Not at all,' he said, and bit into the foot of a Teddy Bear biscuit.

Joe was surprised, considering the stories of terror drilled into children by the nuns. 'You're not scared that you could burn in Hell? Forever?'

'Never. Seeing as I don't believe in Hell,' Charlie explained, 'it's not at all possible for me to be afraid.'

Joe was astonished. 'You don't believe in Hell?'

'No God would be so cruel as to create such a place.'

Charlie wiped crumbs from his beard. 'Let's get back to work,' he said, before detecting the look of puzzlement on his grandson's face. 'Don't be so shocked, Joe. It's what I believe. Maybe I shouldn't go against what you're taught in school, but I think it wouldn't harm you at all to feel the same way as I do. When I was a boy at school with the nuns, I was fed the same tales they use to frighten you children today. It wasn't long after I was out of school that I escaped the horror stories for good. I'd had more than enough of them.'

'Why?' Joe asked.

'Because I was sick and tired of the cruelty.'

Charlie put his empty glass on the ground, picked up a final length of copper pipe and threw it in the back of the wagon.

'Do you believe in Hell, Joe?' he asked. 'That's a more important question as far as I'm concerned.'

'I think I do. The priest and the nuns talk about Hell all the time.'

'I'm hardly surprised,' Charlie said, shaking his head. 'When a person feels a need to tell the same story time and time again, there's a need to do so, to convince themselves it's all true. In most cases, it most likely isn't. Let me ask you another question. This story of Hell and eternal suffering, it puts fear deep inside you, doesn't it?'

'Yes,' Joe said. 'I don't want to burn forever. Sometimes I can't go to sleep at night because I'm afraid if I was to die in the night, and I haven't been to confession to get rid of my sins, I'll wake up burning in a fire.' The thought of such a punishment brought tears to the boy's eyes.

Charlie put an arm around his grandson to comfort him. 'None of that will happen to you, Joe. Why do you think you get into so much trouble at school, right under the noses of the nuns who tell such terrible stories? You're never in trouble with your mother. Or with me.' Charlie patted his grandson on the head. 'You're a wonderful boy at home, Joe. Always.'

Joe struggled with the question. Charlie felt a need to help him with the answer.

'You may not know it, Joe, not yet, but you're a stronger boy than I was at your age, and a lot smarter too. I believe what you're doing is testing yourself. Testing them nuns as well. Maybe you were even testing God with that painting your face trick. Do you understand what I'm saying?'

'Not really,' Joe said, overwhelmed by the thought that he would dare test God.

'Let's leave this be for now,' Charlie said. 'It's a heavy topic, for sure. Anytime you feel a need to ask a question about any of this, I'll be ready to listen. Nothing worse than having trouble like this on your mind and feeling that you have no-one you can speak with. One day, sooner than you might think, you'll make your own choice about Heaven and Hell, and the rest of what them nuns throw at you. It will be your decision. Not mine. And not that of a priest or nun.'

Joe had a final question for his grandfather. 'If you stopped believing in God, why did you send my mum to the church school?'

'That's a good question,' Charlie said. 'Reason

number one is because your grandmother was the staunchest of Catholics. All her life. And Ada made the decisions around your mum and your aunty, Oona. I would never have sent them to the church school, but Ada was not a woman to cross. Number two, I didn't say to you that I don't believe in God. Your grandfather is somewhat of a slow thinker and I still have a decision to make on that issue, even at my age. I gave up on the church a long time ago. But not God just yet.'

The tailgate of the station wagon tilted precariously towards the ground. 'Do you think this car is safe to drive?' Joe asked. 'With all the heavy pipes in the back. We might get a flat tyre, Char.'

Charlie studied the angle of the wagon. 'I think we might be safe,' he answered. 'I've carted a lot more scrap in the back of this vehicle than we've loaded this morning, and I've never experienced a problem. A flat tyre? It wouldn't matter a lot, Joe. If we have to, we can drive on the wheel rim. It's been done before.'

There was little room for Joe to sit in the front of the car. Both the seat and floor were littered with bundles of typed letters and envelopes tied together with string and rubber bands.

'What's all the paper for?' he asked.

Charlie turned the key in the engine with one hand and scratched his head with the other, as if he wasn't certain himself. 'Bills and letters, mostly, I'd expect. I've been meaning to file all this,' he explained, 'but I haven't found the time.'

'Why have you left them in the car?' Joe asked.

'In case the house burns to the ground. These are important documents that I can't afford to lose.'

Charlie guided the station wagon into the back lane. It was a warm morning, and when they drove by the gardens Joe could see that many kids were already at the pool, splashing about. He'd planned to be there with them and should have felt a sense of envy. But he didn't, not at all, to his surprise. He looked across at his grandfather, hunched over the wheel trying to get a better view of the road ahead through the grimy front windscreen.

Charlie whistled a familiar tune as he drove. Joe felt pleased that he'd been ordered to spend his weekdays with Charlie, and not because he would be paid for his work. He loved his grandfather for many reasons, including the fact that he never lost patience with the many questions Joe asked him. Questions that others seemed to have little time for, even his mother, who sometimes chastised him for 'thinking too much'.

'Can I ask you a question, Char?' he said.

'Sure. You can ask a hundred and one questions if you like.'

Joe smiled at his grandfather.

'What's funny?' Charlie asked.

'Nothing, Char. Nothing.'

FOUR

RANJI KHAN'S SCRAPYARD WAS AT the end of a potholed road in the shadows of the city's gasworks. A pair of metal tanks towered over the suburb and could be seen from almost every street corner. It was believed that if either tank were to explode, every home, hotel and factory in the area would be obliterated.

As Charlie drove along the dirt road, in the shadow of the tanks, Joe peered out of the side window of the station wagon. One tank was full, the other empty. Birds looped through the skeletal frame of the empty tank.

'What would happen to us if that tank blew up right now?' Joe asked.

'Well, we wouldn't have to think too much about the existence of Hell,' Charlie said. 'We'd be right in the fire. Sinners, non-believers and the God fearers all. We'd better get a move on.' He laughed and put a little pressure on the accelerator.

They drove through the iron gates into Ranji's yard. If Joe believed his grandfather to be a champion collector, nothing could have prepared him for this. Car wrecks, seemingly of every make and model, were parked on one side of the yard. Next to the cars were cubes of distorted metal, the result of vehicles being crushed in the iron jaws of a prehistoric compactor nearby. Rows of forty-four-gallon drums overflowed with other metal objects: taps, door handles, lead skirting, fire grates and electrical wiring. An ornate spiral staircase stood alone in the middle of the yard, offering a journey to the clouds.

Ranji Khan was standing in the doorway of his office, which was no more than a wooden-framed hut lined with flattened kerosene tins. He was cleaning oil from his hands with a cloth. Ranji wore navy overalls over a flannel shirt and had a red turban on his head. He waved at Charlie before he was out of the wagon.

Joe had heard stories about Ranji from his grandfather but had no idea what to expect on meeting him. Walking across the open yard towards him, Joe stayed close by his grandfather, a little fearful of the man with a heavy beard and strange headwear.

'Good morning,' Ranji said. 'What have you been up to, Charlie? It has been more than a month. I thought you were dead, and you had forgotten to invite me to your funeral. I have been here in the yard cursing your bad manners, while at the same time praying for your safe journey to the other side. But here you are. Back from the grave like you're Lazarus in the Bible.'

'Knock it off. It hasn't been that long,' Charlie said. 'I'm sorry to disappoint you that my heart is still beating like a bass drum.' He theatrically thumped a fist against his chest.

'Where have you been then?' Ranji asked.

'At home, easing into my retirement.'

'And what does this involve?'

'Well, it's a busy life, Ranji. I have the important duty of reading books and falling asleep in my chair. I've dug a new vegetable bed. And just this morning with my workmate here,' Charlie nodded towards Joe, 'I've begun the monumental task of tidying the backyard. As you can see, I've filled the wagon for you.'

Ranji looked over at Joe. 'And this is the grandson you've been boasting about for many years?'

'Yes. This is Joseph Cluny. Marion's boy. Say hello to Ranji Khan, Joe. The undisputed scrap metal king in the whole of Melbourne, if not the entire state.'

Joe lifted a hand and awkwardly waved, fixated on

Ranji's headwear. 'Hello,' was all that he could manage.

'Hello to you,' Ranji said. 'Are you a collector like your grandfather? When Charlie comes to visit me, his wagon is loaded with scrap metal. He then leaves with the odds and ends that nobody wants. Not even me.'

The two men laughed. Joe wasn't sure what to say.

The scrap man smiled at him. 'Children. You talk too much. Or you are silent. Me and your grandfather, we do not stop talking when we meet up. The Ranji and Charlie show. It's never-ending.'

'Never-ending bullshit,' Charlie added.

Joe looked across to the rows of forty-four drums.

'Would you like to see what I have gathered?' Ranji asked. 'Let me make a deal with you, young man. This will be our first business transaction. We scrap men are always making deals. If you find something that you like in the yard, you can take it home with you and begin your own collection. Any item that you can carry out without assistance from your grandfather, you can keep. Go and look.'

Ranji and Charlie unloaded the station wagon together and stacked the scrap metal on a set of industrial weighing scales. 'He is a good boy?' Ranji asked.

Charlie's eyes lit up. 'Oh, he's a beauty. Joe's a daydreamer and I love that about him. Gets himself into some grief at school. And he has some inventive ways about him. Copped a belt earlier in the year for painting his face black.'

'Really?' Ranji mused. He smiled slightly. 'My mother used to paint her face white, with the make-up. She wanted our family to fit in.'

'Did it work for her?'

'Not at all. She could never get rid of her accent and she gave up on the disguise.' Ranji chuckled to himself. 'The nuns were not happy with the boy's black face?'

'They weren't. It would be no surprise. They're only happy when they're unhappy.'

'They must be happy often then. I collected from the convent one time, where they live behind that high wall. The scrap iron from a rusted laundry roof had to be taken away. To this day I have never seen more miserable faces. Like … what are the words you use, Charlie?'

'I have no idea what you're talking about.'

'Like the smacked arse. That's it.'

'I guess you don't look in the mirror of a morning?' Charlie said. 'Your own face isn't so pretty.'

'If I were not a devout man, I would curse you,' Ranji said.

'Well, thank God that you are. I wouldn't want you testing our friendship with blasphemy.'

Ranji checked the weight of the scrap metal on the

scales, took a pen from his pocket and scribbled a figure on the sleeve of his overalls. 'Come into the office. I will make tea and we can settle on a price.'

The pair sat together in the office drinking tea and catching up with old men's gossip. The scrap metal business was both a closed shop and a dysfunctional family, and Ranji Khan found much to complain about, particularly others in the business who he claimed were always undercutting him on the price of copper, the scrap man's gold.

In the yard, Joe moved from drum to drum, searching for possible treasure. Little attracted his eye until he noticed a large wooden crate sitting behind a drum overflowing with metal pram wheels. The chest resembled the pirate's treasure he'd read about in books. He opened the lid. It contained brass hinges, locks and keys. About to close the lid, Joe spotted what appeared to be the end of a barrel in a bottom corner of the chest. He reached inside, tugged on the barrel and managed to free it. Joe was surprised to be holding a gun in his hand. A revolver. It was rusted, and one side of the wooden grip was missing. He looked over his shoulder to see if anyone had seen what he'd found, stuck the revolver down the front of his pants and covered it with his t-shirt.

*

Ranji Khan checked his watch and excused himself. 'Pour yourself another cup of tea,' he said to Charlie. 'I will be only a few minutes.' He collected a hessian sack draped over the back of his chair and left the shed. He walked to a corner of the yard and laid the mat on the ground beside an open tank filled with a murky liquid. It had a putrid smell.

Ranji didn't realise Joe was standing nearby until he'd finished his prayers. He stood and folded the sack. 'Have you been watching me pray?' he asked.

'I'm sorry,' Joe said. 'I didn't know what you were doing.'

'You do not have to be sorry. I was having a few words to myself. Do you pray?'

'Every day, at school,' Joe said.

'I do also. Why do you pray?' Ranji asked.

'Because the nuns tell us to.'

'That is the only reason?' Ranji asked.

'And I don't want to go to Hell,' Joe said.

Ranji shook his head. 'That is not a good reason for prayers. Your grandfather tells me that you are a good boy. Do you enjoy working with Charlie?'

'I do.'

'Can I give a Catholic boy some advice?' he asked.

Joe supposed that if an adult wanted to give him advice, he had no choice but to accept it. 'Yep.'

'You should think less about Hell and more about happiness.'

'That's what Char told me this morning,' Joe said.

'Then, your grandfather is a wiser man than I would have given him credit for.' Ranji chuckled to himself. 'In fact, he is also a good man. Do not tell him I said so.'

Joe stared into the tank. It was the size of a small swimming pool. The pungent scent irritated his nose, causing him to sneeze.

'Bless you,' Ranji said.

'What's that for?' Joe asked.

'That is a stripping bath,' Ranji explained. 'Every scrapyard must have one. This one contains my own formula. I use it to strip the cloth sleeve covering electrical wire. I put a roll of scrap wire into the tank of a night before I lock up. The next morning, when I return and pull the wire from the tank, all that is left is the precious metal. Copper.'

'What's in the formula?' Joe asked.

'Certain acids and sodas. I'm sorry, but I cannot divulge the exact recipe to you. Every scrap man has his own formula. Mine is known as Ranji Khan's Brew. There's nothing that my tank cannot strip.'

'Nothing?'

'Exactly. If a man was to fall into the tank at night, by the following morning he would be finished.

Except for his bones, of course. And in a week, the bones would be gone also. I know this for a fact.'

Joe doubted that the scrap man was speaking the truth. 'A fact?'

'I feel that you don't believe me,' Ranji said. 'Then let me tell you a story. A true story rather than one of your grandfather's wild tales. One night, some years ago, my yard was broken into by a pair of thieves. They wanted to get into my office where I keep the safe. The men were seen by the security guard from the gasworks next door. He telephoned the police, and the men attempted an escape. One of the thieves was caught, but the other one, he disappeared into the darkness somewhere around this location. The man was never seen again.'

'What happened to him?' Joe asked.

'Nobody can say, not for certain. It was a mystery. Weeks later I was sitting in my office, when I realised he most likely fell into this bath. By then, there would have been nothing left of him to show he was ever in the world. Months later, when I was fishing a roll of copper wire from the bath, I found a small length of bone, human I believe, entangled in the wire.'

The liquid bubbled and a veil of steam rose from the surface of the tank. *A ghostly spirit*, Joe thought, backing away.

Walking across the yard, towards Ranji and Joe, Charlie called out to his grandson. 'It's time for us to go. We've more jobs at home.' He looked into the tank. 'I see Ranji has introduced you to his cauldron. And I bet he's told you how long it takes to strip a man of his bones? The story of the missing thief?'

'He did,' Joe said.

'Well, don't pay too much attention to him. Ranji calls on that tale to put fear into kids. It's a trick of his, isn't it, Ranji? Frightens children just enough that if one of them ever had an idea to break in one night, the thought of being spooked by a dead robber would be enough to frighten them off.' Charlie patted his old friend on the back. 'If nothing else, you're a great storyteller, Ranji.'

'As are you,' Ranji said. 'That's why I like your company, Charlie. Young Joe, has your grandfather told you about the talking dog that tragically refused to speak when it needed to most?'

Joe had heard many stories from Charlie, but never a talking dog story. 'I don't know that one,' he said.

'Then you must ask him to tell you. Charlie's stories are always well told, but unfortunately, none of them can be believed,' Ranji said.

'And you're telling me that your stories are true?' Charlie asked, appearing genuinely offended.

'Of course they are. When a man tries to steal from another, or hurts another person without reason, he must be punished for his crimes.' He pointed towards the tank. 'In this instance by having his body boil away to nothing. There is a necessary truth at the heart of such a story. And an important lesson.'

'If you say so,' Charlie said. 'In future I'll remember not to cross you.'

The men hugged and said goodbye to each other. Joe had never seen one man touch another in such a way. He felt embarrassed, without knowing why he should feel so. Joe got into the passenger seat of the wagon. The barrel of the rusted pistol dug into his thigh. Charlie wanted to stop at the bank on the way home and deposit the money Ranji had paid him for the scrap metal.

'Do you want one of those tin moneyboxes they have?' he asked. 'Now that you're a worker, you'll be able to save money.'

Joe thought of the stolen moneybox sitting in the bottom of his wardrobe and hoped Charlie hadn't sensed any guilt. 'Yes please,' he said.

Joe watched Charlie go into the bank and sat in the car imagining that he was a bank robber in a western movie. He thought about the type of mask he'd wear, to go along with the gun stuck down the front of his pants. He wouldn't use a handkerchief over his face. Or a lady's stocking.

Ruby had once ordered him to put a stocking over his head and play the role of a robber in a game she'd created. Joe was supposed to break into her house through a window. She would discover him in the dark, hit him over the head with a rolling pin and kill him. The game didn't get far. When Joe drew the stocking over his face, his nose and lips flattened so badly that he couldn't breathe. In a panic, he tore the stocking from his head and refused to try on a second one, despite Ruby's attempt to coax him into doing so.

Remembering Ranji's story of the missing thief and the acid tank, Joe was backtracking on the idea of robbing the bank when a man approached the car and rested a hand on the open window. He wore a dark suit, open-neck shirt and a greying crewcut.

It was Joe's father, Stan Curtis. He reached into the car and patted the back of Joe's hand. 'How are you, son?'

'I'm good,' Joe said, without looking up. Meetings with his father were tense and thankfully brief for the boy.

'How's your mother?' Stan asked.

'Good,' Joe said, in a flattened voice. Marion had drilled her children to share as little of their lives as was necessary with their father.

'And your sister, Ruby? I heard she's away for a holiday.'

Stan Curtis, like Charlie Cluny, seemed to have a knack for knowing most everything that went on in the neighbourhood, including the movements of a daughter he rarely saw, let alone spoke with. He reached into his jacket pocket, brought out a leather wallet and took a banknote from the sleeve. 'You give this money to your mother and tell her to buy something for Ruby and yourself.'

Joe hesitated. His mother had also instructed him to always refuse money from his father.

'Can I help you, Stan?' Charlie was standing on the footpath. He had a metal moneybox in one hand, in the shape of an office building. The bank's city headquarters.

'Charlie Cluny,' Stan said. He spat out the name, ever resentful that after his separation from Marion she'd not only reverted to her maiden name but had gone to the expense of hiring a lawyer to legally change the surname of her children as well.

'I don't need your help. I'm having a word with my son,' he said, clearly annoyed at Charlie's interference.

'We don't have time for talk,' Charlie said. 'I need to get him home to his mother.'

'You'll have to make time, Charlie. I have business with my boy.' He looked at his wristwatch. 'And we both know there's no hurry for you to get him home to his mother. She'll be at the shop.' He waved the banknote in Joe's face. 'Pass this to your mother. And say hello from me.'

Joe wouldn't take the money. Stan dropped it in his lap, winked at Charlie and walked away.

Charlie got into the wagon and picked up the banknote. He neatly folded it several times and popped it through the slit in the top of the moneybox. 'You keep this and save it. Anytime Stan offers you money, you take it, and you put it in this box.'

'I don't think I am supposed to take it,' Joe said. 'Mum says not to.'

'I want you to take this money. Your father owes you. And your mother and sister also. Your mum is being stubborn. Nothing more than that. One day you'll be able to buy her something nice with the money you save. Her and Ruby both. They deserve it.'

The barrel of the revolver was burrowing into Joe's thigh. He pulled it from his pants and showed it to his grandfather. 'I found this at the scrapyard.'

'A revolver,' Charlie said. 'Where was it?'

'At the bottom of an old chest.'

'Give me a good look at it.' Charlie handled the gun. 'It's in poor condition. I don't expect it could fire a bullet. I know Ranji said that you could take what you wanted, but you should have let him know about this. It might be an antique. There was no need to be secretive, Joe.'

'I thought he'd take it from me,' Joe said.

'There'd be no chance of that. Ranji is a man of his word,' Charlie said. 'He would have let you keep it. But never mind. There's no harm been done. Just think about what I've said.' He inspected the revolver more closely. 'Your mother would be less impressed with you handling a gun than finding out you took money from your father. It's best that you leave this with me.' Charlie tapped the glass on the dashboard clock, doubtful the time on the dial was accurate. 'Let's get home.'

On the drive back Joe asked his grandfather about the talking dog that Ranji had mentioned. 'You want to hear the story now?' Charlie asked.

'Yes please.'

'This is an old story and a true story. Truer than what Ranji told you in the yard, about the burglar in the acid bath. I heard this one from an uncle of mine when I was a boy. It was told to every kid in the neighbourhood. It's a parable. Like the stories in the New Testament. You know what a parable is?'

'From the Bible?'

'It can be. A parable is a story that teaches you to

live the right life. Not a good life necessarily, but the right way to be in the world. Are you ready for it?'

'I am.'

Charlie straightened his back and began the story. 'There was this fella, an old circus man. He'd retired from the ring, and when he left, he took his dog with him. A small black-and-white dog. It was a Jack Russell.'

'The dog's name was Jack Russell?'

'No. I don't know what the dog's name was. That's not the point of the story, Joe. A Jack Russell is a breed of dog. A small and brave dog. What matters here is that the animal could speak. Fluent English.'

'A talking dog?' Joe asked, in disbelief.

Charlie grew a little frustrated with his grandson. 'Joe, when a person is telling a story, your job is to listen. Not interrupt. Okay?'

Joe thought it best not to answer and nodded his head in agreement.

'With no work and no money in his pocket, the circus man was soon down on his luck. He owed cash all over town. One day a debt collector turned up on his doorstep chasing a payment. With interest. Now, everyone hates a debt collector. Dogs included. Another dog was out in the street that day. A big mongrel from the yard across the road. When it spotted the debt collector on the street, the dog charged at him and took a chunk out of the man's leg. Police were called, and the Jack Russell was taken in for questioning. A case of mistaken identity, which seems odd as the offender was a good half-foot taller and seventy pounds heavier than the suspect.'

'The small dog had done nothing wrong,' Joe pleaded, unable to hold his tongue.

'Correct. The Jack Russell was innocent of any crime. He was also the only witness to the incident. All that he needed to do to save his own life was to speak up. And he could speak, as you are already aware. Instead, he lay in a corner of the police cell on the cold ground and said nothing.'

'Why would he do that?' Joe asked.

'Because he knew, as everyone in the neighbourhood knows, human and animal both, that you tell police nothing. Not a word.'

'But if he didn't speak up, wouldn't he be punished?' Joe asked.

'You're right again. And he was punished. The police put the dog down the next morning, at daylight. The Jack Russell was executed for a crime he never committed. A sad ending to his life. It's one reason why, to this day, that I'm against capital punishment, by the way.'

'That wasn't fair on the Jack Russell,' Joe said.

'It wasn't at all,' Charlie mused. 'But the dog died a hero. And that's what matters in this story.'

'He was a hero?'

'He was. Kept his mouth shut.'

FIVE

JOE RETURNED TO CHARLIE THE next morning, again helping his grandfather work in the yard, although it wasn't work as most people would understand it. While Charlie claimed he was on a mission to tidy the shed, to Joe's eyes the project consisted of his grandfather moving pieces of his collection from one side of the shed to the other and then returning the odds and ends to their original place later the same day. Charlie also insisted that they stop regularly for cups of tea, calling for 'steam in the boiler'.

The pair also made regular trips in the station wagon together, 'scouting missions' as Charlie referred to his accumulation of more unwanted goods. In addition to his friendship with Ranji Khan, Charlie had an array of eccentric acquaintances who he'd gathered over the years and regularly called on.

Around once a month Charlie dropped in for a visit to Mr Grainger, an elderly man who'd once been the only dentist in the suburb. He was a generous man and treasured member of the local community. Mr Grainger's motto had always been 'pull first, pay later'. If a patient couldn't afford the cost of an extraction, he would go ahead with the procedure and wait on a payment rather than force a person to endure unnecessary pain.

Over the years, Charlie had supplied the dentist with the fine wire he used in making dental plates. As well as filling and pulling teeth, Mr Grainger had developed a hobby that most people found a little peculiar, if not disgusting. Although he'd retired from the dental profession twenty years earlier, he continued his hobby into his early eighties, having a ready supply of raw material at hand.

Charlie decided to take Joe along with him on a visit. Nothing could have prepared the boy for what he discovered. They knocked at the door and were welcomed into the house by the dentist's youngest daughter, Mona, a woman aged in her fifties, who lived with and cared for her father.

Joe noticed a sculpture sitting on a bookcase in the hallway, next to a desk lamp, that had been fashioned by the dentist years earlier. Further along the hallway, Joe passed a framed mirror, itself another sculpture. In the next room, in the dimmest light, the old man sat in a leather armchair wrapped in a woollen blanket. In front of him on a table was another *objet d'art*, as the dentist referred to the items in his collection. A castle with several turrets and even a drawbridge. It, and other ornaments in the house – many more that Joe was yet to discover – had been constructed almost entirely from extracted human teeth. Baby teeth. Molars. Wisdom teeth.

Charlie introduced his grandson to the dentist. The old man smiled. He didn't have a single tooth in his mouth and Joe wondered if he'd possibly used his own teeth on one of his artworks.

While Charlie sat and spoke with the old man, Mona took Joe by the hand and guided him into another room. 'This is our museum,' she explained. 'My father's creativity needs to be shared. We're hoping to one day open the room to the public.'

Joe looked around the room, lined with shelves containing many more objects made from teeth. One shelf was full of model cars. Another, decorated cottages.

The woman picked up one of the works. 'This is my father's prized work. It took six months to complete and contains many mouthfuls of teeth.'

Joe found himself staring at a model of a human skull made of human teeth, except for its blue eyes, which appeared to have been fashioned from playing marbles.

'Watch this,' the woman said. She manipulated the lower jaw of the skull. Its mouth opened. 'Look,' she said. 'A full set of beautiful teeth. My father set aside the best ones for its mouth.' The teeth were perfectly straight and gleaming white. It seemed odd to Joe that they could have been extracted from a person's mouth in the first place. Mona then showed Joe her own teeth, smiling widely. They were also in excellent condition. 'All my own,' Mona said, proudly.

Back in the station wagon after the visit, Joe was surprised that his grandfather made no mention of what they had both seen in the house.

'Char?' he asked.

'Yep,' Charlie said.

'Don't you think it's a bit creepy all that stuff made from teeth?' Joe asked.

'I used to think so. Then one day I asked Mr Grainger why he did what he did. He was building the model cars back then. He said he began the hobby because he was against throwing stuff out that could be used, which, as you know, is a sentiment I agree with. When he started in the trade, Grainger would throw the teeth away. Until one day, he told me, he stumbled on an idea, out of the blue, that there could be a better outcome for a person's extracted tooth. Art. He began on his first model car the next week. With proper permissions, of course. Mr Grainger has never used a tooth without the good wishes of the patient he's taken it from.'

'Do you think it's strange of him to do that?'

'Possibly,' his grandfather said. 'But no stranger than painting your face black in honour of a moneybox.'

At the end of the day Joe met his mother out front of the dry cleaners and they walked home together. He told her about the visit to the retired dentist and his art collection.

Marion remembered her own trips to Mr Grainger when she was a child.

'Mr Grainger took out two of my back teeth when I was your age,' she said. 'Maybe he used them for one of his sculptures? Did you notice any teeth that could have been mine?'

'I was too scared to take a close look,' Joe said. 'But Char said the dentist never used anyone's teeth for his art without their permission.'

'Your grandfather called what the dentist does *art*?'

'Yep.'

Joe picked up a scuffed tennis ball from the gutter and tried bouncing it. There was little air in the ball and it rolled back into the gutter. 'Do you think Char is lonely?' Joe asked.

'That's a question out of the blue,' Marion said. 'No. I don't think he is. He misses Mum. Every day. I'm sure of that. But I would hope he'd talk with me if he was lonely. Your grandfather keeps himself busy and knows lots of people. He can't walk one street block without being stopped for a chat. What makes you think he might be lonely?'

'When I was leaving the house, Char was setting the table for his tea and it just looked lonely. I thought about him eating on his own and washing the dishes alone. And then sitting in his armchair with no-one to talk to.'

'Your grandfather can always eat at our place if he wants to. He could stay over for the night if he was ever lonely. I'm always inviting him, but he says he's too busy, that there's so much he needs to do at home. Maybe, when you're there tomorrow you can ask him over for lunch on Sunday.'

They arrived home and Marion opened the front door to the house. 'Looks like you've brought most of the dirt from your grandfather's yard back here with you. You'll need to wash and change your clothes before we eat.'

They were sitting at the table enjoying cold roast chicken and salad when they heard a knock at the door. Marion looked up at the clock on the wall, thinking about who might be calling at the house at mealtime. 'I'll bet that's the Salvation Army collecting,' she said. 'They know to turn up around this time of day when people are at home having their dinner.' She took a shilling coin from her purse. 'This should be enough to send them away before they offer me a reading from the Bible, and a holy card.'

When Marion opened the front door, her younger sister was standing on the doorstep. 'Oona,' Marion said, 'what a surprise.' She immediately noticed there was something out of the ordinary in her sister's expression. Oona raised a hand and covered one side of her face.

Oona was six years younger than Marion, who'd been Charlie and Ada's only child until the year she started school. Oona's arrival was the result of an unexpected pregnancy. Having suffered two miscarriages in the years between the births of her two daughters, Ada was certain that Oona was a blessing from God and that she was a special baby, *gifted* even. She was born with a full head of black hair and a lively expression. She was a stunning-looking baby. Each fortnight, at the weigh-in at the Infant Welfare Centre, other mothers urged Ada to enter her in a baby contest. 'There's cash to be won,' one of the mothers chimed, 'and a year of free nappies.' Ada, a private person in every way, wouldn't hear of what she called 'a pantomime for show ponies'.

Oona quickly developed an independent spirit. Even as a young child she spoke up for herself and was forever attempting to break away from the secure hand of her mother. By the time she was a teenager she drew trouble, on the street and in school. Oona had no fear of the nuns, priests, the terrifying language of the church or anyone who attempted to contain her. Always willing to defend herself, she would fight on the street against both girls and boys. Oona was fearless.

She was also her father's favourite. If Charlie did see wrong in his younger daughter, he let it pass, preferring to count her wild streak as a blessing. 'She'll never be stood over,' he liked to boast to his workmates at the council yard. Meanwhile, Marion, always the dutiful daughter, was the well-behaved older sister, and eventually a surrogate mother.

Ada first became ill the year Oona turned fifteen. She would spend several years between her bed at home and a hospital ward at Saint Vincent's before she passed away. Oona had left school at sixteen for a job selling beauty products in a department store in the city. After her mother died, a week before her twenty-first birthday, Oona argued constantly with her father, unable to recognise the deep grief that had immobilised him. She left home soon after and moved into a flat with another girl from the department store.

Two years later she began dating a smooth-talking older man, Ray Lomax. Like some urban Prince Charming he swept her off her feet. Although he worked and lived in the same suburb as the Cluny family, Ray was different from the boys and young men Oona had grown up around. He had his own retail business, selling electrical goods from a shop on the main street. He dressed in expensive suits and owned a flat on the other side of the gardens, far enough away from the factories and hotels, in the only pocket of the suburb that a real estate agent would dare refer to as 'exclusive'. Ray had manners and money and Oona could hardly believe her good fortune.

When Marion first met him, she understood why women might find Ray attractive, but was never deceived by his performance. Oona had brought him around to her sister's house for tea one night, to show him off to the family. Marion didn't take to him at all.

Ray talked too much for her liking, and she noticed that he preened himself in the mirror above the fireplace in the front room each time he passed by, as if to reassure himself that he was a peacock. Although Marion hoped the relationship wouldn't last, one look at Oona told her that it was unlikely to end anytime soon. She'd fallen deeply for Ray and had been blinded by the shine. Within months, the gloss had worn off the relationship and Oona's spark was gone.

The evening Oona knocked at her sister's front door her face was heavily made up with foundation, rouge and eyeliner. Regardless, she couldn't mask the shadow of a deep bruise under her right eye. Marion hadn't missed the damage and opened her mouth, about to speak before checking herself. She knew instinctively that, initially at least, she'd have to go along with Oona's charade.

Experience had taught Marion that when dealing with troubled women in the family, at work or on the streets, silence was a necessity, and accusations, even anger directed against a man responsible for a broken face, could be fatal if the truth was ever to be discovered. A single word in the wrong place could be received as a statement of failure. Patience from loved ones, often seething with anger, or gripped by sadness for the victims of violence, was an inherited skill.

'This is unexpected, love,' Marion said, as casually as she could manage, walking ahead of her sister along the hallway. 'Is there something up with you?'

'Nothing really,' Oona replied, her voice evaporating as she spoke. 'I felt like a walk and thought I'd come by for a cup of tea.'

Oona was in no doubt that her older sister had seen through her disguise. Her only wish at that moment was that Marion would not force her to speak the words that would break her spirit even more.

Joe looked up from his dinner plate at Oona and smiled. He was always happy to see her.

'Hello, beautiful,' Oona said.

'Hello, Oona,' Joe said, seemingly oblivious to the bruises on her face.

'Are you hungry?' Marion asked her sister. 'Let me fetch you a plate.'

Oona cradled her stomach as if she was about to be sick. 'I'm not hungry. Just a cup of tea would be nice.' She appeared unsteady on her feet.

'Please sit down,' Marion said. She wrung her hands, anxious about what she should say. She would need to find a way to raise the issue of Oona's bruised face but couldn't do so with her son in the room.

'If you've finished your chicken, Joe. You might want to go to your room,' she suggested.

'Let him stay here,' Oona pleaded.

One step ahead of her sister, Oona knew that as long as her nephew was in the room with them, she'd be able to hold any inquisition from her sister at bay. She stood behind Joe's chair, wrapped her arms around his shoulders and kissed the top of his head.

'You'd love to have a cup of tea with your aunty, wouldn't you?' She winked at Marion with her damaged eye. 'And a biscuit.'

Marion filled the kettle and Oona clung to Joe. He felt dampness on the side of his neck and could hear his aunty sniffling. She kissed him on his cheek and sat down. Joe could see a single tear hanging from an eyelash. It rolled down the side of Oona's face, leaving a trail in the powdered foundation she'd applied earlier. He looked across at his mother, to see if she'd also spotted the tear, but Marion was busy brewing the tea with her back to the table. Joe thought Oona looked just as beautiful as Ruby had on the morning she left home for the holiday. They had similar dark hair and Ruby shared Oona's eyes. Large, deep brown in colour with hazel flecks exploding around the pupils.

Oona reached across the table and took Joe's hand. She squeezed it so tightly he felt pain. When Marion brought the tray carrying the teapot, cups, milk, sugar and the plate of biscuits, she noticed Oona's free hand was shaking, and her mouth was open slightly. It was as if she was wanted to speak but couldn't do so.

Marion shooed Joe out of his chair. 'I need you out of this room. Now. Watch some television. Or go to your room and read a book.'

'I don't want to read a book,' Joe protested.

'Yes, you do. Go now.'

Joe took two biscuits from the plate and went to his bedroom. He left the door ajar and tried listening to the conversation in the kitchen. He could hear Oona weeping and felt fearful of the sounds she was making. Joe went to the wardrobe and took out the metal moneybox. He sat it on the bed and gazed into the eyes of the black-faced boy.

'Do you want to hear a story?' he asked, before retelling Charlie's tale of the talking dog. The moneybox boy appeared to follow his every word, Joe was certain of it. By the time he'd finished the story he could no longer hear Oona crying. He left the bedroom and stood by the doorway leading into the kitchen. Oona was speaking to his mother in a hushed voice and Joe couldn't make out a word of what she was saying.

That evening was the only time Oona had come

to Marion carrying undeniable marks of Ray Lomax's violence on her face. While she wouldn't openly admit to Marion that she'd been assaulted by her boyfriend, Oona understood she could not easily deceive her sister. Previously, she'd avoided contact with her family following trouble with Ray. She'd usually wait until the smashed windows and vases had been replaced and the bruises on her body had faded.

Marion believed that Oona wouldn't have turned up at her house that night unless she feared for her safety. It would be her job to make her sister feel welcome without raising the stakes. 'The house feels a little empty with Ruby away,' she said. 'Why don't you stay over and keep me and Joe company until she's back?' she suggested. 'You can go to work from here, on the tram.'

'I'd love that,' Oona said, without hesitation, itself a surprise to her sister. 'And there's no need to worry over work. I'm off for a few weeks. Holidays. It's quiet in the store after Christmas. Half of us are on the break.'

Marion called to Joe to join them in the kitchen. 'Oona has decided to stay with us for a bit. She's going to have Ruby's bed while she's away.'

When he walked into the kitchen, Oona reached for Joe and pulled him towards her. 'Are you okay with that? Me, having a holiday with you while Ruby is off milking cows? Or whatever it is that she's up to.'

Oona's eyes were swollen and raw, and Joe realised there was something terribly wrong but was afraid to ask what it was. 'It would be nice if you stayed,' was all that he could manage.

Oona struggled to her feet, shuffled into the front room, and curled up in front of the television, wrapped in a blanket. Marion followed her and sat with her arms draped around Oona's body. Joe sat in an armchair on the other side of the room resting a book in his lap. He tried reading but couldn't concentrate. A little later Oona stood up, excused herself and went to bed. Joe moved to the couch to sit next to his mother and they watched a movie together. Joe missed the ending of the film, falling asleep with his head in his mother's lap.

A little while later Marion poked him gently in the ribs to wake him. 'It's bedtime. You need to be ready for your grandfather in the morning.' She wrapped her arms around her son and whispered, 'I love you.'

Joe said goodnight and went to his bedroom. Oona was standing in the middle of the room, studying her body in a mirror that sat above Ruby's dresser. Wearing only a pair of underpants, she examined a deep wound on her side. The sight of bruises, cuts and welts shocked Joe more so than seeing his aunty near naked. He froze. Oona cupped her breasts in her hands. 'Close your eyes, Joe. I need to put something on.'

When Joe was given permission to open his eyes, Oona was standing in the same position wearing a white slip. 'I'm so sorry,' she said. 'This is your room. I should have known better than to parade around without my clothes on.'

Joe was staring at the bruises and cuts on Oona's arms and shoulders. He looked down at her legs. One knee was badly grazed, and blood wept from the wound. He was unable to move or speak.

'Do the marks on my body frighten you?' Oona asked.

'Yes,' Joe whispered.

'Is it me who frightens you? Or the bruises?'

'I don't know,' he said. He wanted Oona to cover her body so he wouldn't have to look at her wounds.

'Come over here.' Oona held out a hand. Joe hesitated. 'Take my hand,' she pleaded. She reached forward and entwined Joe's fingers with her own. 'Don't be afraid of me. You know I'd never hurt you, don't you?' She kissed Joe's fingers. 'These marks on my body,' she said, 'they'll be gone soon.'

'What happened?' he asked.

Oona wasn't sure how to best answer. She was no longer certain herself about what had gone wrong in her life. *What happened?* The question made little sense to her. 'I truly don't know,' she said. She touched a deep bruise on her arm. She had a puzzled look on her face, as if she had no idea what had caused her harm.

'All I know,' she finally answered, 'is that I used to be happy and I'm not happy any longer. Something's gone wrong but I just can't work out what it is.'

Oona felt she might shrink away until there was nothing left of her. Or she could explode with anger. She wasn't sure which outcome she feared more. She wiped the back of her hand across her mouth. 'Can you do me a favour tonight?'

Joe thought his aunty might want him to pray with her. One evening, in the week before his grandmother had died, Joe had stood at the side of her bed and Ada told him to never forget to recite his prayers of a night. 'God listens more closely to children than he does to adults,' she'd explained. 'Most adults are beyond help, in my opinion.'

When Ada was in one of her stern moods, as she was that evening, Joe felt uncomfortable around her. He was too young to know that she was dying at the time and wanted to leave the bed that the family had gathered around.

'Let me tell you, Joseph, no person I ever met got any smarter as they grew old,' she added. 'Don't you ever forget that. You're probably as intelligent now as you'll ever be. It could be backwards from here.'

'What do you want me to do?' Joe asked Oona.

She pulled the blankets back on Ruby's bed. 'You like stories, don't you?'

'Yes,' he said.

'Hop into the bed with me and let me tell you a story.'

'Are you going to read to me?' he asked.

'No. I'm going to tell you a story from memory. One I've always loved. Your grandfather used to tell this same story to your mum when she was a small girl. And then Marion told it to me.' Oona patted the mattress. 'Now, it's your turn to hear it.'

Joe wondered if he was about to listen to another telling of the talking dog story. Or one of the inherited family stories his mother had told him when he was younger. He switched off the bedroom light and hopped into bed alongside Oona. She began the story of a young girl, Lena, who had run away from home to join the circus. She was unhappy at home and believed that by joining the circus she'd discover a life of freedom and adventure. Joe hadn't heard the story before and enjoyed it. But before Lena had reached her destination, Oona was asleep, breathing lightly on the back of Joe's neck.

He lay on his side in the darkness and thought about Oona's answer to his question about the wounds on her body. He couldn't understand what could have gone so wrong in her life for Oona to have been hurt so badly. Joe felt helpless. He remembered back to the day when Ruby had told him that he was never to ask about the wounds on a child's body at the swimming pool. He had never really understood why. He could only think that it must have something to do with suffering and sin but could not imagine who it was that Oona had sinned against.

SIX

Early the next morning Joe was woken by the sounds of his mother working in the kitchen. Oona was in a deep sleep with one arm draped across his chest, and he was staring at a deep cut on her wrist. The wound was beginning to scab. Desperate to go to the toilet, Joe lifted Oona's arm and slipped out of the bed. The kitchen was now empty, and he could hear the tap running in the bathroom. Joe called out 'morning' to his mother, opened the back door and headed across the yard, along the brick pathway that ran between the house and the toilet. He stood in the gloom of the toilet for some time after he'd had a pee. There were questions he'd decided to ask his mother about Oona. He wanted to know if her boyfriend, Ray, had caused her injuries, even though he understood it was something he would normally be forbidden to ask.

When he returned to the kitchen, Marion and Oona were seated at the table talking quietly to each other, just as they had the previous night. Two pieces of toast and a cup of sweetened tea had been placed on the table in front of his chair.

'I've left the toast for you to butter,' his mother said. 'And I've opened a tin of jam.'

Joe sat down, slurped from his hot mug and smothered a slice of toast with butter. Oona's face was in a worse state than the night before. Her blackened eye had swollen so badly, she couldn't see out of it. Joe watched closely as she picked up her cup. Her hand shook and she spilled tea onto the tabletop. She slowly put the cup down, leaned forward and licked the tea out of the cup as a cat would do when drinking milk.

Joe could no longer look at his aunty in such a state. He quickly finished breakfast, went to his room, dressed for the day and waited for his mother on the front verandah. The shift change at the iron foundry across the street was in progress. The same number of men who shuffled wearily out of the metal turnstile, after a night's work, shuffled in for the day shift. It was difficult to distinguish one worker from another. They looked equally worn out. While many local men had been employed at the iron works, Charlie Cluny had once turned down an offer of a well-paid union job inside the foundry, preferring work as a streetsweeper. He enjoyed the outdoors, being in the fresh air, away from the noise and regimentation of the factory floor. He liked to refer to himself as an *independent man.*

Marion came out of the house wearing a fresh uniform. She took Joe's hand in hers and they walked to the end of the street and around the corner to Charlie's house. Marion was unusually quiet until they reached Charlie's front gate. 'You have another wonderful day with your grandfather,' she said.

'Will Oona be staying with us again tonight?'

'Yes, love. She'll be with us for some time. She can't go …' Marion quickly changed the subject. 'If Charlie takes you out in the wagon today, don't you be talking too much. He's a terrible driver and if he loses concentration he could kill you both.' She put a hand on Joe's shoulder and gently prodded him towards the gate.

He held his ground, wanting to ask a question. 'Is Oona being punished?'

'Of course not. Why would you say such a thing, Joe?'

'Because I saw her arms and legs last night. The bruises and scratches and the blood.'

Marion leaned forward, until she was at eye level

with her son. 'Oona has been hurt. But it has nothing to do with punishment. I don't know where you would get such an idea. Now go. Please.'

Joe persisted. 'Jesus was punished,' he said. 'When he was put on the cross. With the nails in his hands and the crown of thorns around his head. And he was speared in his side. His body was beaten, and he was punished for our sins. When I do something wrong at school, I get punished with the strap. What did Oona do wrong?'

'Oona has done nothing wrong,' Marion insisted. She cupped both hands around her son's face. 'And I'm going to have words with the school about giving you the strap. It's going to end.'

Joe doubted his mother would be any match for the ferocity of Sister Mary Josephine and her black leather strap.

Marion tugged at her son's t-shirt. 'I don't want you telling lies, but I think it's best if you don't speak to your grandfather about Oona coming over last night and staying with us,' Marion said. 'Not today, at least. Later in the week I'll sit down and talk to him about Oona.'

Joe didn't welcome the pressure of keeping such a secret from Charlie. 'Why shouldn't I tell him about Oona?' he asked.

'Because I don't want him to worry?'

'What will he worry over?' Joe asked, although he suspected he knew the answer.

'That's too many questions from you.' Marion kissed him on the cheek. 'I'll be late for work if I'm here any longer. I'll see you tonight.'

Joe again worked in the yard with Charlie during the morning, stopping occasionally for their regulation tea break. Charlie was surprised at how quiet his grandson appeared. Each question he asked was met with a short 'yes' or 'no', a shrug of the shoulders and little more. He tried lifting Joe's spirits with a new story, without success.

All the while, Joe was thinking about his grandfather's crystal-ball ability to read his mind and see into his heart. His mother's request had left him feeling anxious. He didn't want to break her trust but knew that if Charlie asked him a question and he lied, he'd be found out. Each time Charlie opened his mouth to speak, Joe expected the words he didn't want to hear. The less responsive he became, the more acute was Charlie's suspicion that something was wrong with the child.

They ate lunch together in the kitchen. Sausage rolls that Charlie had made himself. Once they'd cleaned up and put the dishes away, Charlie brought his chair alongside his grandson and sat down.

'So, Joe Cluny, tell me this. What is worrying you today?'

Joe let out a slow breath, like a deflating balloon, surprised by a feeling of relief now that the question had finally been asked. 'I want to tell you something, but it has to be a secret, Char.'

'That's fine by me,' Charlie said. 'I love a secret.'

'Only a secret between you and me,' Joe insisted. 'Not Mum.'

'As long as you haven't done something bad, it will be fine. If you're in serious trouble, I would not be able to keep something like that from your mother. It wouldn't be right of me. Are you in trouble, Joe?'

'No. I'm not,' Joe said. 'I promise.'

'Good. That's out of the way then. Tell me this secret,' he whispered.

Joe hesitated. 'It's about Oona.'

Charlie frowned. He'd not been expecting a response that would involve his younger daughter. 'What does this brooding have to do with my Oona?'

'She's come to stay at our house,' Joe said. 'She's sleeping over.'

Charlie felt pain in his chest. Oona would only be staying with Marion if she was in some difficulty. 'When did she come by?'

'Yesterday. At tea time.'

'I suppose your mother told you not to talk with me about it?'

Joe instinctively closed his eyes. 'Yes,' he said.

Charlie had no doubt that Oona's trouble would involve Ray. Like his daughter Marion, he'd never been persuaded by the man's charm and had remained uneasy about him. He was aware that Ray had inherited an electrical goods store from his father, but knew little more about him. Charlie made enquiries and found nothing, except for the useless information that Ray Lomax was apparently a talented dancer.

'How was Oona when she came by?' Charlie asked.

Joe didn't want to speak about the marks he'd seen on Oona's body. 'She was tired when she came in and went to sleep early, in Ruby's bed.'

Charlie sensed that his question made Joe feel uneasy. He decided he'd visit Marion's later in the day and speak with Oona personally.

'We'll leave this for now and get back to work. I'm grateful to have you with me again. I wouldn't get through these jobs on my own. Are you ready for a restart?'

Joe was relieved by the change of subject. 'I'm ready, Char.'

★

Late in the afternoon, Charlie insisted on walking Joe home. 'Do you have a key to the door?' he asked.

'No,' Joe said. 'I climb the side gate and get in through the bedroom window.'

'Really? I think we'll try something more conventional.' He knocked on the front door. There was no answer. 'You said Oona was resting?'

'Maybe she's gone to the shops?' Joe suggested. 'Or out for a walk?'

Charlie knocked a second time. 'Has your mother ever spoken to you about giving you a key to your own house? It would make life easier.'

'Char,' Joe said. 'I hear someone.'

The sounds of footsteps walking the length of the hallway were followed by the snap of the lock and creaking hinges. Oona opened the door wearing a faded chenille dressing-gown that belonged to her sister. She grasped the collar tightly at her neck. She looked from her father to Joe and frowned, annoyed that he'd obviously talked to his grandfather. Charlie could see that Oona had several broken fingernails and scratches on the back of one hand. Without the disguise of foundation, the bruising on her face could not be hidden.

'Can we come inside?' Charlie asked.

Oona moved aside and let her father into the house.

He walked into the kitchen, put the kettle under the tap and placed it on the gas stove. Oona stood on the other side of the room, her arms wrapped protectively around her body.

Charlie fussed about, keeping himself busy as he gathered his thoughts. He measured scoops of tea leaves, took cups out of the cupboard and matched them with saucers. He wanted to scream out with anger. Only a day earlier he'd boasted to his grandson that he knew *everything* that went on in his neighbourhood, sometimes before it had happened.

As he filled the teapot with boiling water, he thought to himself, *I know nothing.* He cursed, muttering 'fuck' under his breath. He slammed the kettle onto the stove. *I know nothing about harm done to my own daughter.* He poured the tea into the cups, gathered himself as best he could and asked Oona to sit at the table with him. 'Please come over here. We need to talk.'

Joe, standing behind Oona, rested a hand in the centre of her back, wishing he'd not said a word to Charlie about her staying over at the house.

'No, Dad. We don't need to talk at all,' Oona answered from the other side of the room. 'There is nothing to say.' She was in no mood for a lecture from her father about how she'd made a mistake with Ray Lomax.

'We do need to speak!' Charlie yelled.

He slammed the table with his fist, with enough force that the teacups lifted in the air and spilled tea across the wooden surface. The eruption shocked the three of them. Joe had never heard his grandfather raise his voice. Oona felt fearful of her father for the first time in her life. It was an alien feeling. Charlie appeared bewildered by his own behaviour. His face had darkened so much that for a moment Joe couldn't recognise him. Charlie looked down and watched the spilled tea bleed into the grain of the wood.

'I'm sorry. So sorry,' he whispered. He walked over to the sink, carrying the teacups and saucers, and rinsed them under the tap. He wrung out the dishcloth and methodically mopped up the mess.

'Please, Oona,' he asked again, after cleaning the table. 'Please sit with me. For just a few minutes, at least.' He gestured to a chair with a hand.

Oona moved hesitantly forward and took a seat. Joe sat on the step dividing the kitchen and hallway.

Charlie ran his hands through his head of silver hair and sat down. The faded blue, yellow and streaks of red on Oona's swollen face made him want to cry. 'I am sorry for my outburst.' He looked over at his grandson. 'I need to apologise to you also, Joe. This is unforgivable of your grandfather, the way that I've just behaved. What I have done is terrible. I'm sorry.'

Although Joe had been surprised by his grandfather's outburst, he didn't believe there was any reason for Charlie to ask forgiveness of him. Whatever his grandfather had done, Joe was certain it was no sin.

Charlie took Oona's hands in his. 'Please tell me. What has happened to you?'

'Joe shouldn't hear this conversation,' Oona said.

'But he needs to,' Charlie demanded. 'He's been anxious all day, fearful of not only what he can't say, but what he doesn't know. We can't have him damaged by secrecy. It's a poison. We all need to know the truth, Oona. Please tell me.'

'I can't,' Oona said. 'There's nothing to say.'

Charlie frowned. 'Nothing? That can't be. Your fella, Ray. He did this. I know that much in my gut. Why has he hurt you?'

'Why not, Dad?' Oona answered, with anger of her own that surprised her father.

'I don't understand you,' Charlie said. 'Why would you say that?'

'There's nothing special about me, Dad. Jesus. And why are you so shocked?' Oona said. 'Look at what you just did in your own daughter's home. Slammed your fist into the table. Shouting. This is your answer to a man laying into a woman. Screaming at your own flesh and blood? Putting fear into your own grandson?' She pointed an implicating finger directly at her father. 'I'll tell you why not. Because it's what you do. Men. All of you. Do you know any woman or any child around here who hasn't been harmed?'

Oona sat back, feeling emboldened and surprised by her criticism of her father.

'I do know,' he said. He pointed to the kitchen floor. 'Here. In your own sister's house. And two streets away, in the home you were raised in.' He called Joe to the table. 'You must tell Oona now. Has your mother ever hit you? Have I ever harmed you, Joe?'

'Leave him out of this, Dad,' Oona said. 'And he wouldn't be hit in this house because there's no man living in it. Joe. Go to your room,' she snapped. 'Your mum wouldn't want you hearing this.'

Charlie persisted, again raising his voice. 'You tell your aunty.' He thumped a fist against his own chest. 'Joe. Have you ever been hurt by anyone in your family? I need you to tell the truth. For Oona. She needs to know.'

'Get out of here. Now!' Oona screamed at Joe.

In that moment, Joe feared both his grandfather and his aunty equally. All he wanted was for them to stop shouting at each other. He stood up. 'No-one has hurt me, not at home,' he said, 'only at school.'

'What did I tell you, Oona,' Charlie said, ignoring Joe's final comment. He rested an open hand against his daughter's injured cheek. 'There is no "why not" in this family. No-one has the right to hurt you. It stops now. I won't have this from Ray.'

The tenderness of her father's touch immediately softened Oona. He looked so distressed, she believed he was about to break. 'Dad,' she whispered. 'I know you care. But there's nothing you can do. You're an old man and you can't stop him. I need to sort this out for myself. People around here don't interfere. You know that.'

'And how will you sort it out?' he asked.

'What do they call them men that you can hire to do a murder?' she asked.

'What are you talking about?'

Oona smiled. 'Nothing. I'm just being funny. Trying to, at least. A hitman. That's what they call them. There must be plenty of hitmen around this neighbourhood. Maybe we could put all our money together and hire one of them fellas to kill Ray.'

'Is that the only plan you have?' Charlie asked.

'For now, it is,' Oona said.

Charlie ignored the flippant comment. 'How long will you be staying here?'

'I don't know for certain. I have the bed until Ruby is back home. After that, I'm not sure where I'll go.'

'Well, I know. You'll come and live with me,' Charlie said. 'You will take the big room, mine and your mother's room.'

Although she would never admit it to her father, the idea appealed to Oona. From the day she'd walked out of her parents' home she'd missed the love it held for her, particularly her memories of when she was a child. Her mother wasn't given to outward expressions of love, and yet her daughters had always known that she would do all she could to care for them. Each time she went back into her parents' house, Oona was comforted by a scent both indescribable and familiar, reassuring her that she was home.

'And what about you, Dad? Where would you sleep if I took your bed?' Oona asked.

'Where I sleep now. In the reading chair under the window in the kitchen. With my books and my teapot. The open fire in wintertime.'

'Why don't sleep in your own bed?' Oona asked.

'Because I never do,' Charlie said.

'That's not an answer, Dad. How long have you been doing this?'

'From the day after your mother passed. The evening she was laid out on the bed.'

'But I was there for months after she died and never found you asleep in the chair.'

'Why would you?' Charlie said. 'I was up by four of a morning and at the council yard by five. You were always sound asleep.'

The thought of her father retreating to an armchair in the kitchen saddened Oona. 'You haven't slept in your own bed? Not once?'

'I did sleep in the bed beside your mother on the night she died. I rested a hand on her shoulder and stayed awake through the night, trying to convince myself she would come back to me. The next morning, I looked at her body and knew she was gone. I'd finally drifted off to sleep early in the morning and she'd snuck away on me. With your mother gone there's never been a thought of sleeping in that bed.'

'And you think I would want to sleep there?' Oona asked. 'In the same bed where my mother died?'

'Maybe not,' Charlie said. 'But it's a better prospect than going back to a monster. Will you please think about this? Talk it over with your sister for me?'

Charlie stood, went to the kitchen sink and looked out of the kitchen window to the afternoon sky. Oona was right. He would be no physical match for Ray Lomax and had none of the criminal connections that might otherwise be called upon to persuade a man to change his ways. He turned and again apologised to his grandson. 'I'm sorry for what has happened here,' he said. 'I promise you, Joe, that I will never behave this way again.'

He walked across to the table and placed an arm on his daughter's shoulder. 'If your mother was alive, she'd demand that something was done. She might start with a prayer, but if trouble persisted, if more harm was done to her children, Ada wouldn't stop until it ended.'

'And how would she do that?' Oona asked.

'I'm not certain how. But I know that she'd find a way. Whatever it took, Ada would act. Without hesitation.'

SEVEN

AFTER BEING TOLD ABOUT OONA'S argument with their father in the kitchen, Marion thought it best to leave Oona to settle. She'd ask no questions about Ray Lomax and what Oona's plans were to escape him. To lift their spirits, a few nights after Oona had arrived at the house, Marion opened the record player that sat in the corner of the kitchen and brought out her collection of forty-five records. She sat a large wooden box on the table and asked Oona to pick a song that she would like to hear.

'I have at least a hundred records here. Choose whatever you like.'

Oona flicked through the collection, stopping occasionally with a record in her hand, sharing a memory with Marion and Joe of when she'd first heard the song, including a tune she'd once listened to while having her hair set at Marilyn's Beauty Salon on the main street: 'Downtown' by Petula Clark. Another, first heard through the speaker above the make-up counter where she worked was 'Be My Baby' by The Ronettes.

'If you tell a story for every record I have in that box,' Marion said, 'we won't get to hear a single song.'

Oona finally selected a Beatles record, 'And I Love Her'. Marion put the forty-five on the turntable and sat down. With the opening 'I give her all my love ...' Marion and Oona began singing. They both had beautiful voices and, despite their age difference, had similar tastes in music. Joe knew the song – his mother played it often. While he was too shy to sing along with them, he hummed in harmony with the women, their sweet voices filling the room.

They played music for the next hour or more and sang every song, word for word. When Joe was offered a choice of music, he picked out Peter, Paul and Mary's 'Puff the Magic Dragon'. It was Ruby's favourite; she was also a wonderful singer.

'I love this one,' Oona said, when the song began. She clapped her hands in time to the beat and sang as loudly as any voice had ever been heard in the Cluny kitchen.

Marion joined in during the chorus, followed by Joe. When the song had ended, the three of them smiled at each other and sat with the shared quietness, no-one saying a word.

Marion called for 'last song', which was a family tradition. She again asked Oona to choose something. 'You're our guest. The closing number must be yours. Make it something special, sis.'

Oona went through the collection a second time and eventually chose an old seventy-eight sitting at the bottom of the box. 'I want this one,' she said, handing the record to Marion.

Marion smiled at her sister. 'That's a wonderful choice.'

The song, 'Wheel of Fortune', was performed by Kay Starr. It had been a favourite of their mother's. She'd owned the very copy Marion held in her hand and could sing the tune beautifully with a voice as magical as Kay Starr's own. All the Cluny women enjoyed singing at parties. Although she never volunteered to perform, Ada would eventually be called on to stand in the middle of the room and entertain the family with a number before the night was over and 'Wheel of Fortune' was her signature tune. There'd never been a need to teach the song to her daughters. They'd come to know all the words, simply by being around their mother and listening to her voice.

Marion flicked the switch on the record player to the seventy-eight speed. She changed the needle and carefully lowered the arm to the edge of the rotating black surface of the record. A familiar crackle filled the room, followed by the sound of a lucky wheel ticking over, and then the brass section of a big band.

Oona stood up and smiled. 'Can we dance to this one?' she asked Marion.

'Yes please,' Marion said, bowing theatrically to her sister. 'I spend too much time in this kitchen dancing alone.'

Marion put one hand on Oona's shoulder and the other around her waist. The women slowly circled the kitchen table with Joe watching them. He noticed the sparkle in his mother's eyes and the smile on Oona's face that he'd missed since she'd arrived. Just for a moment her bruises appeared to have vanished.

When the song ended, the women continued to hold on to each other. Oona rested her head on her sister's shoulder. Marion put the record collection away and they went into the front room, shared the couch together and watched television.

In bed later that night, Oona again told Joe the story of Lena, the girl who ran away to join the circus, and this time they reached the end without Oona falling asleep. While Lena had been attracted to the excitement of the bright lights, the music and the performances, she realised she missed her home and family and decided that she needed to run back to them. When she arrived, she discovered that the house was empty, and Lena thought she'd been abandoned. She sat on the doorstep in despair. A few minutes later the family returned home. Her parents, a brother and sister, and her pet dog.

Joe enjoyed the story so much he persuaded Oona to tell it once more from the beginning.

The following morning a postcard arrived in the letterbox from Ruby. On the front of the card was a photograph of a pen of sheep. Joe wondered if it might have been Ruby's job to round them up. If sheep herding was the highlight of his sister's holiday, Joe was glad that he'd not been chosen. On the back of the card Ruby had written that she'd been learning to ride a bicycle and paddle a canoe in a dam behind the family farm.

'Your sister is having a wonderful time,' Marion said, after reading the card.

'Not as good a time as I'm having with Char,' Joe responded.

Marion knew how close her father and Joe were. Even still, she was a little surprised at his comment. 'So, you like getting dirty every day rather than going to the swimming pool with your friends?'

What Joe did like was finding a rusted gun in a wooden chest, meeting an old man who made art out of teeth, another who wore a red turban, listening to his grandfather's stories and drinking endless cups of tea. Charlie's refusal to accept the existence of Hell had almost convinced Joe there would be no need to attend confession and admit to Father Edmund that he'd stolen the moneybox boy from the classroom.

'Yep, Mum. I like to get dirty.'

When Joe arrived at Charlie's the next day, his grandfather and Ranji were in the backyard, sitting at a workbench. Charlie was busy polishing the metal barrel of the gun with a ball of steel wool. The six-bullet cylinder had been removed from the revolver and Ranji was meticulously tending it with a pipe cleaner. The men were talking animatedly to each other, heads together, until they spotted Joe in the back doorway. They stopped abruptly, as if they were withholding a secret, Joe thought.

'What are you doing with the gun?' he asked.

'Just what it looks like,' Charlie said. 'We're cleaning it. We've discovered that this revolver is an antique, and Ranji believes there's good money in it. We're going to cash in and sell it.' Charlie detected the disappointment on Joe's face. 'With your permission, of course. Seeing as you found it, Joe, you're entitled to full share of the sale price. The earnings will be split three ways. Equally. After all, we three are now business partners.'

Joe wondered if selling the gun would constitute a sin? And if it was then used to commit a major crime, would selling it amount to a mortal sin having been committed by the sellers of the revolver as well as the criminals who used it?

'We do not need to sell it immediately,' Ranji said. 'We could possibly shoot a person first. We are waiting to see if the opportunity presents itself. It is the only way to truly test the operation of the revolver.'

'Who would you shoot?' Joe laughed.

'That is an excellent question,' Ranji said. 'What do you think, Charlie? Who should we shoot?'

Charlie looked to be deep in thought, as if he'd taken the question seriously. He said nothing and continued cleaning the barrel.

'Do you have bullets for the gun?' Joe asked.

On cue, Ranji reached into a side pocket of his overalls and slapped a handful of bullets on the workbench. 'There they are. Six in total. One for each cylinder. They are thirty-eight calibre. The same as the gun, fortunately. I've had these for over twenty years. I would like you to guess where I found them,' he said to Joe.

'In the gun?'

'No. I didn't know I had the gun until you found it in the trunk. The cylinder had been so clogged with dirt it couldn't have held any bullets at all let alone fire one.'

Ranji held the cylinder in his hand and examined each compartment.

'It's clean as a whistle now.'

He held a bullet between a finger and thumb.

'This I found inside a book. Can you believe it? I picked up two metal cabinets on the side of the road many years ago. They were locked and I had no key. But I didn't care, as they were going to scrap. When I got the cabinets back to the yard and hauled them from the rear of my truck, I could hear something shifting around in one of the drawers. I thought that possibly there was an item of value inside. I picked up a pinch-bar and jemmied the drawer. Inside were books and nothing more. Can you believe it? Who would lock books away in a cabinet? What a crazy idea is that?

'I picked up one book, opened it and found that

someone had cut into the pages and made a secret compartment. The bullets were sitting there. I was going to throw them away but changed my mind, thinking *you never know.*' He smiled at Joe. 'And now, you find a gun that matches the bullets. A good collector knows what to keep and what to dispose of. It's an instinct. I have it. Your grandfather doesn't quite have it, as he has little idea what to rid himself of. But I think you may have it, Joe. You know what is of value that can never be thrown away.'

Joe thought about the moneybox boy and realised they would always be together.

'What book was it?' Charlie asked.

'I beg your pardon?' Ranji said.

'The book? What was the title? The one with the compartment for the bullets.'

Ranji looked at Charlie with disbelief. 'What sort of question is that? I have no idea what the title of the book was. I was interested in the bullets. Not the book.'

'And you've kept them for over twenty years?' Charlie asked. 'Even though you had no gun.'

'At least twenty years,' Ranji said.

'They might not fire at all,' Charlie said. 'This gun could explode in your hand, it's in such poor condition.'

'Maybe you could shoot it?' Joe offered. 'Test it, Char.'

'I don't think so,' Charlie said. 'I'm fond of my hand and I don't want my fingers blown off. Even if I did fire it, I doubt that I'd hit anything. By the time I'd practised my aim well enough, I'd be out of bullets.'

'To be truthful, I do not need to shoot this gun to get a fair price,' Ranji said. 'I know that it will bring us good money.'

'Who will you sell it to?' Joe asked.

'We will sell the revolver to people who like shooting other people.'

Both men laughed aloud. Joe wasn't sure if they were joking. Several men had been shot on the streets of the suburb over the years, and the stories of their violent lives were folklore. Schoolchildren liked to stop and poke a finger into a neat hole on the sandstone wall of the post office. It had been created many years earlier when a local criminal fired at an enemy one warm summer night. The first bullet missed its target and lodged in the brickwork. The second bullet killed a man.

Charlie handed the revolver to Ranji. He reassembled the cylinder and rotated it. It spun like a well-oiled wheel. 'It works perfectly,' Ranji said. 'Next, we need to repair the wooden grip.'

Joe couldn't take his eyes off the gun. He desperately wanted to pick it up and feel it in his hand. He also wanted to point it at a target and shoot. Charlie opened a drawer below the benchtop and brought out an oiled cloth. He wrapped the pistol in the cloth and returned it to the drawer. He noticed the excitement on Joe's face. 'You're never to touch this gun. Do you understand me?'

'Yes,' Joe answered, realising yet again that his grandfather appeared to know what he was thinking without him uttering a word.

Ranji collected the bullets and returned them to his pocket. 'It doesn't matter too much if the boy touches the revolver,' he said to Charlie. 'On its own, it's harmless. All that we need to do is keep the gun and the bullets out of each other's company until the time comes to sell it.'

EIGHT

WITH OONA'S HEALTH GRADUALLY IMPROVING, she began to think about leaving Marion's house. As the bruises on her body faded, so did the memories of what she'd experienced at the hands of Ray Lomax. Many times she'd managed to find excuses for not only Ray but herself. Ruby would be coming home from her holiday at the end of the following week and Oona would use her niece's return to reason that she could not impose on Marion any longer.

Marion was horrified when Oona told her about her decision. 'Please don't do this,' she said. 'I want you to stay as long as you need to.'

'But Ruby will be home soon, and she will want her bed back.'

'Ridiculous. She'll be happy to share with you. We

can put a set of bunks in the room if we need to. Or you can sleep in with me. Please don't leave, Oona. You're not ready.'

Oona sensed the anguish in her sister's voice and attempted a joke. 'I can't sleep in with you. You snore.'

'And so do you. We'll complement each other.' Marion laughed. 'At least think about it. If you won't stay with me, then I want you to take up Dad's offer to live with him for a while. You'll have your own room around there and I'm close by if you need anything.'

'I can't stay with Dad. He'd drive me mad.'

'He's not so bad,' Marion said.

'I'd bet you couldn't live with him. There's so much clutter in that house. Just finding a teaspoon takes half a day.'

'Do you have a better plan?' Marion asked, frustrated with her sister.

'I could take a room in a boarding house,' Oona said.

Marion laughed at the idea. 'Where there's no-one to look out for you? What if Ray comes after you? Who'd stop him, Oona?'

'He won't come looking for me,' Oona said, doubting her words even as she spoke. 'And who do you expect would stop Ray if he came here? You or me? No chance. And Dad? He's not up to it, at his age. As it is, he's too gentle for a fight, thank Christ.'

Marion struggled to admit to herself that Oona was right. 'You need somewhere better than a boarding house.'

'It will be good enough for me. I'm due back at work in a couple of weeks and need to be settled. I don't even have my shop clothes here with me. As it is, I'll have to go back to the flat and collect them, whatever I decide to do.'

Marion clasped her hands together in thought.

'Are you praying for me now?' Oona asked.

'Not quite,' Marion said. 'But, seeing as you mentioned prayer, I do have an idea.'

In an act of desperation, Marion managed to persuade Oona to join her and Joe at the following Sunday mass. She loaned her sister a pale blue dress, a pair of black shoes and a veil. Walking from home to the church, neither woman appeared enthusiastic about what they were about to do.

Joe strolled between them, wondering what his mother was up to. That Sunday morning wasn't Easter, Christmas or Ash Wednesday, which were the only days of the year Marion usually attended mass, except for the occasional funeral. Ruby and Joe went to church each Sunday without fail, as they had little choice. Sister Mary Josephine watched over the congregation from the choir balcony and stood on the steps of the church after mass, recording the names of every student in attendance. If a child was regularly absent from mass a letter, seeking an explanation, was sent home to the family. Or more foreboding still, Father Edmund sometimes visited religiously wayward households and interrogated the parents of children.

The church was full that Sunday morning. If not deeply religious, the local community were tribally loyal. Joe spotted several classmates he hadn't seen since the end-of-year break-up. Each of the children looked a little older since Joe had last been in school. He avoided eye contact with Sister Mary Josephine, fearing that she might suspect him of kidnapping the moneybox boy. Joe paid little attention to Father Edmund's sermon and absentmindedly forgot to drop the coin his mother had given him on the donation plate. She glared at Joe after the plate had passed them. He'd been too busy daydreaming, thinking about Ruby and wishing he was on the farm with her, paddling a canoe instead of having to sit through a sermon. Each time a prayer was recited aloud Marion joined in with a clear voice, putting on a show for the priest, whereas Oona barely raised a whisper. Nor did she bother to kneel or stand when called upon by the priest, preferring to rest in the pew and yawn.

When the priest stood at the altar, with his back to the congregation, preparing the wine and hosts for communion, Joe sat up and paid attention. Father Edmund raised a large host above his head, followed by a goblet of red wine. With the announcements, 'This is my body … this is my blood,' a shiver pulsed through Joe's own body, as it did each time he'd heard the words from the day of his first communion four years earlier.

When the time for communion arrived, he knelt next to his mother at the altar. The elderly men of the congregation stood in the aisle behind the women and children until their own time came.

Father Edmund stood in front of Joe and recited the words, 'Body of Christ.'

Joe answered 'Amen' and the host was placed on his tongue. It stuck to the roof of his mouth and slowly melted. He watched the priest walking across the front of the altar, placing hosts in the mouths of the parishioners kneeling before him. Although he understood that it was wrong to think so, the ritual had always reminded Joe of placing ping-pong balls into the mouths of smiling clowns at a carnival.

Following mass, Father Edmund left the church. He was trailed by a procession of altar boys and nuns from the school. People filed out of the church and past the priest, who acknowledged them on the worn stone steps at the front. He occasionally spoke with a parishioner, with a sense of formality that assured them he had no interest in a lengthy conversation.

Once Marion was outside the church, she took Oona's hand and pulled her towards the priest. Oona attempted to resist her sister.

'Good morning, Father,' Marion said, keeping a tight grip on Oona's hand. 'Thank you for the service today.'

Father Edmund reprimanded her. 'It is mass, not a service.'

'Of course,' Marion replied politely, although she wasn't interested in knowing the difference. 'I would like to have a word with you, please, Father. Both my sister and I.' She put a hand on Oona's shoulder and guided her towards the priest. 'You would remember my sister, Oona? She was a student at Our Lady's many years ago.'

Father Edmund didn't appear to recognise Oona. 'I would rather you come by the church during the week,' he said to Marion.

'I do understand, Father. But I can't come and see you on weekdays. I work. Full-time. As does my sister. If we could have a few minutes of your time now, we would be appreciative. Wouldn't we, Oona?'

Oona was busy examining a scuff mark on the toe of one of her borrowed shoes and said nothing.

'Alright,' the priest said. 'Wait for me at the presbytery door and I will see you soon.'

Joe remained close to the women, intent on hearing his mother's reasoning for speaking with the priest.

Oona was angry with Marion and let her know why as they walked around the side of the church to the presbytery. The pathway was flanked with colourful rose bushes attended to by Mrs Westgarth.

'What do you think you're doing?' Oona asked. 'We don't need to see a fucking priest. I know I don't, at least. I never liked him when I was in school, and I like him less now, with his fucking lecture from the altar. You remember the way he used to press himself against us when we were kids? The man is a creep.'

'Don't call him a creep and please don't swear,' Marion said. 'We're in the church grounds. I don't want you using your tongue that way in front of Joe.'

Oona laughed, a little too loudly for her sister's liking. Other parishioners, leaving the church, stopped to watch.

'You think Joe hasn't heard swearing when he's out on the streets?' she asked. 'On *our* streets?' She turned to her nephew. 'Joe. Can you listen to this, please. Fuck. Fuck. Fuck. And fucking fuck.'

Joe knew he shouldn't laugh but couldn't stop himself from doing so.

'There you go, Marion,' Oona said. 'He's heard it now.'

'Don't you be giggling, Joe,' Marion snapped. 'None of this is funny.' Marion stared at her sister and wondered if she wasn't going crazy. 'You're behaving like a child. I only want to ask Father Edmund if he can help us. There's no reason for you to kick off, Oona.'

'What help could a priest give me?' Oona said. 'Listen to yourself. This is ridiculous. Unless he can convince Jesus Christ himself to come down from the cross and give Ray a decent kicking, there's nothing he or the church can do for me.'

'Please shut up,' Marion hissed. 'People are watching us.'

'Well, they can get fucked,' Oona said, loud enough for the onlookers to hear her. People began moving away in embarrassment. 'And fuck the church,' she added.

'Don't you curse the church,' Marion said. 'It's why we're here. For help. The church has a fund. A charity the diocese supports. It gives accommodation for teenage girls and young women in trouble. The charity helps them find work. Professional jobs. You can get away from Ray and the make-up counter at Myer and make a new start for yourself.'

'I don't need a new start. I like the job I have. And are you really that naïve, Marion? That charity fund is nothing more than a front for stealing babies. Those girls aren't going into any job – professional or in a factory. They're pregnant, for fuck's sake. The church houses them until they give birth and then the babies are taken away from them. All this shit is the church controlling us with lies. How do you think Ruby won a free holiday away?' she added. 'The poor girl. She's had to play the role of Saint Bernadette of Lourdes all year just to get a couple of weeks of sunshine.'

'Keep Ruby out of this,' Marion demanded.

Joe could see the priest marching towards them. 'It's the Father,' he whispered.

The women fell silent.

'What did you want to ask of me?' Father Edmund said. 'My Sunday afternoons are busy.'

Marion again took hold of Oona's arm. 'My sister has a difficult issue, and she needs support, Father.'

'What type of support?' he asked, impatiently checking his watch.

'Well …' Marion hesitated. 'Her … her boyfriend has assaulted her, and Oona needs to get away from him. She will need accommodation and help with work. I know the church supports a charity—'

The priest cut Marion off. 'What do you mean,

"her boyfriend"? You are speaking of her husband, I expect?' he asked, continuing to ignore Oona.

Marion was about to lie on behalf of her sister, until Oona interrupted her. 'He's not my husband. Like my sister said, he's my boyfriend,' she said, smiling at the priest, determined to antagonise him further.

'Your boyfriend,' Father Edmund said. 'Do you live under his roof?'

Joe spotted the anxious look on his mother's face.

'I do live with him,' Oona answered. 'But it's *our* roof that we are under, not his, Father.'

'And he assaulted you?' the priest asked.

'Yes. He hit me.' Oona's response was one of defiance, rather than any desire for sympathy.

The priest looked over at Joe and frowned, annoyed that the boy was present during such a conversation.

'There is nothing I can do,' he said to Oona, waving a dismissive hand in her direction. 'You chose to live in sin with a man who obviously has no respect for you. It is wrong that he assaulted you, in any way,' he added, possibly for Joe's benefit. 'But it is not at all surprising, under the circumstances.'

Father Edmund directed his final comment to Marion, as if Oona had again become invisible.

'Your sister does not require charity. What she does need is religious guidance through confession and penance. If she was a married woman, this would not have happened.' He smiled, not in a courteous manner, but with the superiority of someone assured that he knew what was best for those around him. 'God bless you,' he said, and began walking away.

'Fuck you,' Oona muttered.

Marion's face reddened. She was now as angry as her sister. She called out to the priest. 'Father. Please wait.' He stopped and turned. 'My sister,' Marion pleaded, 'she has been badly beaten by a man, and she needs help. She's done nothing wrong. This is a violent man who has sinned, not my sister.'

'Of course, he has,' Father Edmund said. 'The fact changes nothing. I cannot help a woman who also lives in sin. Not until she attends confession. If you are so concerned for your sister, contact the police, not a priest.'

Marion scoffed at what both she and the priest knew was a ludicrous suggestion. 'Is that it?' she asked. 'Can't you offer her something?'

'As I just explained to you. Confession and penance.'

Marion was fuming. 'Wait, Father. Just one more minute of your time. Come here, Joe. Now.'

Joe reluctantly joined his mother and looked down at a line of ants, marching between the priest's black leather shoes.

'My son,' Marion said, putting a hand on Joe's

shoulder. 'He's not to be strapped at school. Ever again.'

'I beg your pardon?' Father Edmund asked, clearly infuriated.

'Nobody at the school or church, not the nuns and not you, Father Edmund, are to hit my boy again.'

'You cannot ask such a request,' Father Edmund said. 'Corporal punishment is an accepted disciplinary practice in the Catholic system. It is used only as necessary, at our discretion. And your child, who lives in a home without a father, appears unable to avoid trouble. Can you explain what would possess a child to paint his own face with black paint, mocking a charity that supports children of the third world?'

The story about Joe painting his face was true, Marion realised. As would be the cruel act of submerging his head in a bucket of water as a punishment.

'My son wouldn't know what it means to mock anyone. He is a kind boy who doesn't deserve to have his face shoved in a bucket of water.' She took a step closer to the priest. 'I'll take him out of Our Lady's and put him in the state school system if I need to.'

'That is your decision, not ours,' the priest said.

'That's all you have to say?' Marion asked.

'That is all.' Father Edmund walked away, squashing the ants beneath the heel of his shoe.

Marion turned to Oona and clenched her fists.

'What a bastard,' she said. 'The fucking bastard.'

Oona laughed at her sister.

'What's so funny?' Marion asked.

'Your plan. It's worked out so well,' Oona said. 'You dressed me up for church to get help for me from the priest. Instead, I've been cast out as a sinner and your son will likely be expelled from school because you've finally realised that they have no right to belt him. And to top it off, you've ended up swearing at the priest yourself. You've done good work, sis.'

'If you hadn't insisted on telling him that you lived with Ray,' Marion said, 'I might have got somewhere.'

'Maybe,' Oona said. 'And that would take lying to a priest, which would mean that next week you'd be in the confessional owning up to him and I'd be found out anyway. I was only thinking of you, Marion.'

'Why the hell did you paint your face black?' Marion barked at Joe.

In his defence, Joe called on his grandfather's observation. 'I told Char what I did, and he said I painted my face because I was testing God.'

Marion groaned. 'Your grandfather said that? You were testing God?'

'Yep.'

'Well, your grandfather is an idiot.'

★

After the argument outside the church, Marion and Oona settled on an unspoken truce. Later that evening they sat together on the lounge watching television. By the time the late movie ended, Oona had drifted off to sleep with her head on a cushion. Marion looked vacantly at the test pattern on the screen. She was too weary to bother getting up, either to turn the set off or go to bed.

Marion was angry that Ray's violence had impacted so many people. Not only Oona, but herself, Joe and her father. Once Ruby was home, she'd also be drawn into the drama, as she was too sharp a girl to keep any secret from. Born with an inquisitive nature, Ruby would ask questions, and wouldn't be put off until she had an answer. Marion felt sad for her father. Charlie was a gentle man, helpless to protect his own daughter, which left him full of guilt. Only Oona could save herself from Ray Lomax and Marion doubted that her sister would be able to do what was needed.

Marion had known others in Oona's situation. Fresh-faced young women a few years out of school, excited with the idea of getting married, dreaming of a romantic future ahead of them. Marion would occasionally run into the same women on the street just a couple of years later. Their faces had become featureless, and they would attempt to disguise their hollowness with lifted voices and fractured smiles. The exhausted performance would end as soon as the women walked on, shoulders hunched once again, their eyes meeting the ground.

Marion caught a glimpse of her own reflection in the television screen. She couldn't allow herself to escape criticism. In some ways, she felt she'd made a greater mistake than Oona. Marion had not only gone out with a man she didn't love. She'd married him.

Oona coughed and Marion turned to watch her sleeping sister. She looked peaceful. Marion was reminded of the nights when they were younger and would curl up under a blanket watching television.

She gently shook Oona. 'Come on, love. Bedtime.'

Marion helped her sister to her feet. Oona was confused, unsure of where she was. Recognising her sister's face she smiled and said, 'It's you, Marion.' Oona kissed her sister on the cheek. 'It's really you. I've been having a beautiful dream about our mum. Let me tell you about it.'

Marion put an arm around Oona's waist and guided her towards the bedroom. 'You can tell me in the morning when you're properly awake.'

'Oh, I can tell you now,' Oona said. 'In the dream I'd gone to Heaven. And I was back with Mum. It was beautiful, Marion. So beautiful.'

NINE

Charlie called by the house the next morning, unannounced, for breakfast. He again apologised for his outburst a few nights earlier. Oona put her arms around her father's neck. 'That's enough, Dad. You can stop saying sorry. It's over now.'

None of them – not Oona, or her father, or Marion – believed their trouble was over at all, but nothing more was said that morning. The family gathered around the table and talked about the weather, shared Ruby's postcard, and gossiped about Mrs Barker next door, who'd apparently taken in a *star* boarder to help with the rent and ease her loneliness. After breakfast Joe left with Charlie, who talked to him about the jobs ahead of them that morning. He'd decided to 're-order' his book collection.

Standing in his grandfather's kitchen, Joe looked at the makeshift shelving and the many titles crammed in at various angles and couldn't see that they'd been ordered in the first place. The work took them most of the morning, as it required some deliberation from Charlie before placing each book in its rightful position. Not because he found alphabetical order a challenging concept. Each book he owned held a story of its own, and Charlie insisted on telling it. He would hold a book in one hand and caress it with the other. He'd then summarise the work for Joe or reminisce about the first time he'd read it, including where he was at the time and how he felt once he'd finished reading.

'*Captains Courageous*. Now, I found this one way up on a top shelf of the Book Depot that used to be on the corner, next door to the garage. I was in the back room, and I could *feel* there was a book up there on the shelf waiting for me. I climbed the wooden ladder and there it was.' He patted the front cover of the hardback as if it was a pet. 'I could hardly see the gold lettering for the dust covering it. Mr Collins, who ran the shop, he let me have it for free. A novel for free. I could hardly believe my luck.'

'Did you like the book?' Joe asked.

'Oh, I loved it. I love all my books. I was a slow

reader, back then, but I persisted. They're yours too, from now on. You pick any book you like from the shelf and take it home and read it. If I ever get around to writing myself a will, all my books will go to you.'

'What's a will?' Joe asked.

'I guess the best way to describe a will is that it's a statement that lists all your possessions and who you have decided to leave them to after you die. Saves family arguments, some believe. The books, they'll be yours.'

Joe didn't want to think about anyone dying, let alone his grandfather. 'What about your collections in the yard?' he asked. 'Who will they belong to?'

'I haven't decided yet. Let's see what we have left after I've tidied. There'll be something for you. And Ranji, of course. I can't forget him.'

'And your house?'

'Oh, this will go back to the owner, who I pay the rent to.'

'You don't own it?' Joe asked, surprised to hear that another person owned the house that his grandparents had lived in for so many years.

Charlie chuckled. 'No. I don't own it. I've never known anyone around here who owns the house they live in. Not personally, at least.'

At lunchtime Charlie made Joe a tomato and cheese

sandwich. 'I've an errand to run,' he explained. 'You stay here, and if I'm not back when you've finished eating, please shelve more of the titles in alphabetical order, just as we've been doing.'

'I can come with you,' Joe said. 'And help out.'

'I'm sure you could. But I need to do this job alone.'

Charlie left the house and walked to the main street, passing several shops until he reached the dry cleaners. He looked through the window. Marion was standing behind the counter, sorting through cleaning tickets. She spotted her father, he waved and Marion came to the door.

'Hi, Dad. What are you doing here?'

'What time is your lunch break?' he asked.

'Whenever I want it. Why?'

'Can you take it now? I need to talk to you.'

'Sure,' she said. 'Give me a minute and I'll get one of the girls to cover for me.'

They walked to a nearby cafe and sat in a booth by the window. While Marion was surprised that her father had asked her to lunch during a working day, she was sure that the conversation would concern Oona.

'This was always your mother's favourite spot,' Charlie said. 'We had our first proper date at this cafe.

We sat right here in the window. I wanted to show your mother off to the street. She was so beautiful.'

Marion had heard the story of her parents' courtship many times but didn't mind listening to her father reminisce yet again. Memories of Ada brought out the best in him. The assault on Oona had taken a toll on them both. Marion's face was drawn, while Charlie's remained flushed with anger.

'This is a first for us,' Marion said. 'Out to lunch on a workday. Why the treat, Dad?'

'I don't know that this will be a treat, to be honest.' He straightened the tablecloth as he gathered his thoughts. 'I can't sleep, worrying over Oona,' he said. 'And she wouldn't speak at all this morning about what's gone on. Or how she's going to pick herself up. I can't get through to her.'

'It's not you, Dad. She doesn't want to talk to anyone about what happened to her. Oona feels ashamed.'

'Of what?' Charlie asked. 'There's nothing for her to be ashamed of.'

'She believes she's made a terrible mistake and it can't be fixed. And Ray, knocking her around, he humiliated her and she can't hide from that, whether we speak about what's gone on or not. I'm worried she's going to leave my place soon. I can sense it. Once Ruby returns, Oona will use it as an excuse to go.'

'Have you seen Ray about on the street?' Charlie asked.

'No. His shop hasn't been open all week. With a bit of luck, he's disappeared.'

'I doubt it. Not when there's money to be made.'

Marion looked down at her hands resting on the linen tablecloth. She'd bitten her fingernails to the quick. 'Look at these,' she said. 'They're horrible. They look like a rat has been chewing on them.' She placed her hands under the table, out of sight.

'I know it doesn't sound right to say this, but it might be best that she does leave,' Marion said.

Charlie frowned. 'It couldn't be best for anyone. Not for Oona or us.'

'I'm thinking about the kids,' Marion said. 'This trouble has upset Joe. The sadness on his face when he saw the bruises on Oona. It was awful. And Ruby will be home on the weekend. She knows this goes on, but she's never had to deal with it, and I don't want her to have to go through this. Ruby adores Oona. If she'd been at home and seen the state that Oona arrived in, her heart would have broken. I don't want that happening to her. We grew up without this, and I want my kids to have the same.'

'You'd sacrifice Oona for the children?' Charlie asked.

'That's not fair, Dad. Not at all.'

Charlie immediately regretted his words. 'I'm sorry,' he said.

The waitress took their lunch order, and they sat in silence. Charlie was brooding over something more that he felt needed to be said.

'Growing up without this trouble in the house didn't stop Oona from the mistake she's made,' he said. 'Choosing Ray Lomax.'

Marion wouldn't have Oona blamed for what had happened to her. 'Don't be saying that. Ray has the gift and she fell for it. Everyone took to his polish.'

'Not you, Marion.'

'Or you, Dad.'

'One of us should have warned her,' Charlie said.

'Would have made no difference,' Marion said. 'Oona's always been the stubborn one. And look at me. I'm no role model. The decision I made marrying Stan. I knew he was trouble when I met him, and I still said, "I do."'

'Stan's not so bad. Not much of a father, but he's a grafter. Did he ever hit you when you were together?'

'Not once,' Marion said, without hesitation. 'Stan was too busy counting his earnings. His only interests are cash and arithmetic. I couldn't get his attention on anything else. Not me or the kids.'

They quietly ate lunch. Charlie was bothered by a nagging thought and let his meal go cold. Marion watched him fidget with the salt and pepper shakers. 'What's up, Dad?'

His eyes moistened. 'Seeing my own child's face beaten, it got me thinking. Remembering. Women are hit. Kids. We even beat our dogs. My father, your pop, he'd belt my mother if his dinner wasn't cooked right. If his clean clothes hadn't been laid out and ready for work. Men. We're not much good.'

Although Charlie had spoken little about his childhood with his daughters, Marion had heard terrible stories from her mother, about how Marion's grandfather, a man she never met, had terrified his family throughout their life with him.

'You're not like your father,' Marion said.

'I was like him. Almost,' Charlie replied.

Marion wasn't certain what her father was referring to and was fearful to ask him if he'd struck her mother. They sat sharing an awkward silence. Marion had never witnessed violence as a child, and Ada had never spoken of any trouble she might have had with Charlie earlier in their marriage. If Ada had been hit, it would be likely that she would have remained just as silent as other women, Marion thought, gazing across the table.

Charlie broke the silence with a story he felt compelled to share with his older daughter.

'One afternoon, near Christmas, the year before you were born, I got into a terrible row with your mother. I'd been to the work break-up party at the council yard and had a drink. Just a couple of beers. Nothing more. I was never one for a big drink, and I worked out that day that a couple of pots were two too many for me. I had an argument with one of the foremen. He was one of the Farrells. A tough local family. The talk between us got out of hand and we ended up in a fist fight. He could have really beaten me, but instead, Farrell slapped my face like I'd been a naughty boy. He humiliated me in front of the other men.'

A child passing by the cafe stopped and looked through the window at Charlie. The girl put an open hand to the glass and Charlie did the same with his own hand. The girl smiled and walked on.

Charlie continued. 'I got home a little late, Ada was annoyed at me and we argued.' He stopped and took a breath. 'I can't remember to this day exactly what the talk was about.' He paused a second time. 'But I'll never forget what happened next. I looked at your mother and knew I wanted to hit her in the face. I mean, hurt her.' Charlie fell silent.

Marion paused before asking a question, dreading the answer. 'And did you? Hit my mother?'

'In that moment,' Charlie said, 'I knew what my father would have done if it was him. He would have put that woman in her place and kept her there. Shut her up, like he'd done to my mum.' Charlie wiped a tear from his cheek. 'All of them years, when I was a boy cowering in my bed, hearing him beat my mum, although I didn't know it at the time, he'd been teaching me how to be a man.'

'Did you hit my mother?' Marion insisted.

'No,' Charlie said. 'I left the house. I ran, to tell you the truth. Out on the street and over to where the high school is now. By the river. It was an open paddock back then. I must have walked for a few hours and didn't get back home until well into the night.'

Marion's relief was clear. 'And what did Mum say, when you got back home?'

'Not a lot. But I'm sure she knew what I'd been thinking at the time of the argument. Ada could read me like a book. She told me I was a fool to get into a fight at work. She then ordered me to go to bed and told me to wake up in the morning as the good man she believed me to be.'

'And you are,' Marion said. 'You know I can count the decent men in my life on one hand with a finger to spare, if I include Joe, who's only eleven years old.'

'Who are the others?' Charlie asked.

Marion held a hand up and counted as she named the men of trust in her life.

'Well, there's you and Joe, of course. Then, it's your mate, the scrap man, Ranji Khan. I've always liked him. He's a cheeky fella, and a good man.' Marion struggled to think of a fourth candidate. 'Oh, and Ben Flynn from the garage.'

'Benny?' Charlie said. 'He's a great mechanic, but you don't own a car. What's his claim to fame?'

'Let me tell you,' Marion said, gripping the finger she'd set aside for Ben.

One morning the mechanic walked into the dry cleaners carrying a suitcase. Marion hadn't seen Ben or his wife, Denise, on the street for weeks. She was shocked at the sight of him. Ben looked like he'd lost half his body weight and Marion thought he must be seriously ill. Ben sat the case on the counter and opened it. It was full of dresses in a bright floral material. Denise was known for the lively colours she favoured, a little too loud for some. Marion carefully removed each dress from the case. They were stained with dirt and patches of mud. She looked across the counter at Ben.

He leaned forward and whispered, 'She left me.' That was all he said. He waited for the dry-cleaning ticket, then without another word walked out of the shop.

A week later Ben returned and collected his laundry. 'We managed to get all the stains out,' Marion told him. 'They're as good as new.'

Ben thanked her and left the shop in a hurry, again without saying anything more.

A few weeks later Marion saw him outside the bank. Ben looked a little healthier. He asked Marion if she would sit with him on the bench. 'I'd like to explain myself,' he said.

'You don't have to,' Marion said. 'It's not my business, Ben. The dresses are clean. There's no harm done.'

Ben was insistent so Marion sat with him, and he told her that he'd come home after work at the garage one afternoon to find a note on the kitchen table. Denise had left him and taken only one leather suitcase with her. He went into their bedroom, opened the wardrobe and emptied it of the clothing she'd left behind. He carried an armful of dresses into the yard, threw them in the dirt and stomped on them. It rained that night and by the next morning the dresses lay drowning in puddles of water. Ben looked out of the kitchen window at the damage he'd done then walked around the yard gathering each garment. He draped the dresses over the kitchen chairs to dry before taking them to the cleaners. After he'd collected them, he drove to Denise's mother's house and dropped the dresses off for his wife.

'Why did you do that?' Marion had asked him.

'I'd sat looking at those dresses, cursing myself for having ruined them. It was wrong of me to do that. No woman looked more pleased with herself than Denise did wearing one of her dresses.'

'Was she pleased to have them returned?' Marion asked.

'I don't know. She wouldn't come out of the house and speak to me. I don't really know how to say this in a proper way. I was angry with her, and I still am. But throwing her beautiful dresses in the dirt was the wrong thing to do. I loved her in those dresses, and I still do.'

Her story finished, Marion sat back and waited for her father to speak.

'So, he's another good man?' Charlie said.

'Yeah. I think he is. But he doesn't have a lot of competition, Dad. You are a rare breed.'

*

After lunch with Marion, Charlie headed home with memories of his father's violence haunting him. Although he'd spoken with Ada about his childhood, Charlie had withheld some stories too horrific to speak of from his children. His father was the hardest of men. As a result, Charlie's mother became fearful of showing affection towards her children in front of him. There was no love in the house. The wire-framed bed in the room next to where the children slept groaned like clockwork, early of a Sunday morning. Whatever the sound was, Charlie knew it had nothing to do with affection, as afterwards his mother would sit in the kitchen wearing a face of despair for the remainder of the day.

Charlie had feared his father from an early age and would not allow himself to forget the day he also realised he despised the man and later prayed for his death. It was his eighth birthday, and Charlie found an abandoned kitten in the back lane behind a house they were renting. He brought it into the kitchen and gave it a bowl of milk. Convinced that the kitten was a mystery birthday gift to himself, Charlie walked to the local butcher shop and bought a half pound of sausage meat from savings he made working as a paperboy.

While he was away up the street his father arrived home from work and noticed the kitten playing in the backyard. He filled the laundry trough with water, picked the kitten up by the scruff of the neck and drowned it. Not long afterwards, Charlie returned home with the parcel of meat and searched all over. When he couldn't find the kitten, he asked his father if he'd seen it.

'I haven't seen any kitten,' his father said. 'But if I do, I'll foot its arse.' Charlie noticed that there were bloodied scratches on his father's hands and knew that he must have hurt the kitten.

Charlie found the dead kitten the next morning, in the laneway behind the house. Its fur was still damp, and its body had stiffened. Charlie cut a cardboard box in half, said a prayer over the animal's body and buried it in a corner of the yard, in an unmarked grave to be sure his father didn't find the animal, dig it up and again throw it away. Charlie later confronted his father, accusing him of killing the kitten. His mother, who overheard the conversation, quickly left the house with Charlie's three siblings, and did not return until after he'd had a caning from his father and had been sent to bed without his tea.

Years later, Charlie asked his mother if she remembered the incident. 'I don't remember that at all,' she said, and even suggested that Charlie had dreamed up the story.

Charlie couldn't believe that his mother could have forgotten such a terrible act. 'How can that be, that you don't remember?' he asked her.

'Because it's what I choose,' she answered. 'Once I was free of your father, I found a way to forget. You should too, Charlie. The man was poison.'

Charlie stopped at his front gate and considered the prospect that his mother might have been right all along. Memories of his father, the death of the kitten and his unresolved belief that he'd perhaps inherited the violence of his family were at times unbearable thoughts to contemplate.

Charlie found Joe asleep in the reading chair with a book resting in his lap. He couldn't have pictured a more pleasing sight. Having done poorly at school, Charlie started work when he was little more than a child, and spent his teenage and early adult years convinced he was stupid. He resented education and any person who'd had one. He grew up believing that educated people felt they were better than him, whether they told him so or not.

Sweeping the streets of his own neighbourhood, Charlie was known by most people and was well liked. Passers-by often stopped and talked to him, and he was always available to do favours for others. Warning a laneway bookmaker that police were on the beat. Keeping an eye on a pet dog while a shopper went into the grocery shop. He'd once sat for an hour with a young woman in distress. Her older brother had recently died, run over on his way home from work, and she was heartbroken.

On weekends, when he was a younger and fitter worker, Charlie took on an occasional extra shift in the city centre, sweeping and collecting garbage when the half-day shopping was over. As he cleaned up outside the department stores, people took no notice of him, let alone stop for a word. He was left feeling worthless.

Although he'd read as a child and loved the feel of a book in his hand, Charlie was labelled a 'struggler' and would always be so, according to one of the nuns, Sister Mary Margaret, who ran the school library at Our Lady's when he was a boy. Frustrated at being a slow reader as a teenager, he lost patience with himself and stopped reading altogether. His return to books began after his marriage to Ada, when he picked up a box of discarded paperbacks in a laneway. 'Cowboy novels', they were called. Charlie took the books home and sat in the yard the following weekend reading, slowly at first. As he moved through the stack, his reading improved.

He began to read more quickly and always had something to say to Ada about a book once he'd finished it. Charlie's library grew, as did his tastes. He came to enjoy reading just as much as he loved collecting, and not only for the easier stories he came across. Charlie realised that reading challenged his thinking. His world, until then, had been confined to the gridded streets of his daily life, having rarely moved beyond them. Whereas, between the pages of a book, his understanding of a world beyond his own expanded.

Charlie's reflections were interrupted by his grandson waking. Joe sat up, surprised he'd fallen asleep.

'Catnapping?' Charlie asked. 'It's a good way to cheat a working day.'

Joe closed the book and showed Charlie the cover. '*Tom Sawyer.* Can I borrow this one?'

'Borrow it? I wouldn't think so. You take it home with you and start your library with that one.'

'Ruby has her books in the shelves at home,' Joe said. 'There's not much space left.'

'We won't let that stop us. I'm sure I have a set of shelves in the yard that we can fix up for your bedroom.'

A few minutes later, the scrap man knocked at Charlie's side door.

'Ranji,' Charlie said. 'I hadn't seen you in ages.

Look at us now. We've caught up three times in a week. Would you like to move in with me? I can make up a bunk for you.'

Ranji smiled. 'I haven't come to see you, old man. I'm here for young Joe.' He put a hand in his overalls pocket and retrieved a metal yo-yo. He placed the toy on the table, in front of Joe. 'This is for you. It's as good as anything you will discover in your grandfather's collection. Superior perhaps.'

'Thank you,' Joe said. 'Where did you find it?'

'I didn't find it. This yo-yo I purchased. You found the rusted pistol and we have recommissioned it to make a cash fortune for the three of us. In time, of course. But for now, I felt that we owe you.'

While the two men worked on the final details of the gun, repairing the wooden handle, Joe attempted several tricks with the yo-yo without success. Ranji had brought one of the thirty-eight-calibre bullets with him. When they finished fixing the handle, Ranji spun the cylinder to check that it continued to run freely. He took a handkerchief from his pocket, opened it and laid it on the table. He and Charlie looked down at the bullet as if it was a gold nugget.

'I believe that we should put the bullet into the cylinder to be certain that all is in working order,' Ranji said.

'I don't think so. We can't fire the gun,' Charlie said. 'Not around here.'

Ranji spoke with the patience of a father talking to a distracted son. 'You are correct, Charlie. We will not be firing this revolver in the kitchen. Or the backyard. Any person would find your suggestion reasonable. What we can do is put the bullet in and see that the cylinder still spins freely. If the gun passes this test, we will be able to claim that it's in *perfect working order.* Those three words are the most important for any salesman when advertising a second-hand item.' He held the revolver in his hand. 'Only then will we be able to demand a premium price.'

'You should be selling used cars,' Charlie told him.

'I don't think so. I am a businessman, not a charlatan.'

Ranji passed the pistol to Charlie, and he inserted the bullet into the cylinder, locked the revolver then handed it to back to Ranji. 'I think it's best if you check it.'

Ranji spun the cylinder again. 'Listen to that sound,' he said. 'This revolver is now in perfect working order.'

TEN

Marion was serving a customer in the shop when she spotted Oona walking hurriedly by the window. She asked one of the other workers to take her place and set off after her sister. She passed Ray Lomax's electrical shop further along the street. A 'closed' sign was attached to the front door and a display of newly designed portable radios and record players sat in the window. They were little bigger than the size of a telephone book.

Rushing to the next corner, Marion was about to call out to her sister, but stopped once she realised where Oona was heading, struck by the realisation of what Oona was up to. Marion hunched forward with pain, as if someone had punched her in the stomach. She desperately wanted to scream out. At Oona. To the street and neighbourhood. *Stop!* But she couldn't manage a sound. Marion resumed her pursuit of her sister at some distance.

Oona left the main street and walked in the shadow of the imposing brick wall of the four-storey shirt factory that dominated the block. Over many years the factory had employed women living in the surrounding area, working shifts around the clock. Oona entered the gardens and walked along the wide path lined on each side with elm trees. Marion followed her. It was the same route that Ruby and Joe took to and from the pool, just as their mother and aunty had done before them when they were young.

Oona left the park, headed along a narrow lane and stopped outside a block of flats. Marion sprinted across the road and raced after her sister. She caught up with Oona and stood between her and the pathway leading into the building. 'Please, sis. You don't have to do this,' she said, breathing heavily. 'There's no reason that you have to go back to him. We can work something out.'

Marion noticed that Oona's face was beautifully made up – with mascara, foundation, rouge and lipstick – with no visible signs of damage.

'You've been following me, Marion. Jesus.'

'I have. Because I want to help you.'

'I don't need your help. I want to do this,' Oona

said. 'It's going to be better between Ray and me from now on.'

Marion pulled at her sister by the arm. She'd heard the same comment too many times, from many women.

'Better? It can never be better, Oona. And you shouldn't need me to tell you so. What happened last week, it's happened before, and it will happen again. There's never a better time with men like Ray Lomax. You go back into that flat and the only guarantee you'll have is more pain from him.'

'You don't even know Ray,' Oona countered. 'You've never liked him, and you've never given him a chance. You and Dad both. It's no wonder he gets angry.'

Marion shook her head in dismay. 'Ray was angry? That's what you call it? This isn't about his anger. It's all about a man who thinks he owns you, Oona. A man who believes he has a right to treat you like a piece of dirt. A man who enjoys using your body for a punching bag.'

'You don't know what you're talking about,' Oona said. 'Ray came to the house this morning and we had a good talk. He's made promises.'

Marion was furious. 'Ray Lomax was in my house?'

'Don't worry yourself. He didn't step inside your

place,' Oona said. 'We spoke out the front on the street and I believe what he told me.'

'What is there to believe?' Marion asked.

'Ray said he's going to give up the electrical shop and get a new job. We might even move away. Make a fresh start interstate.' She leaned forward and kissed her sister on the cheek to silence her protests. 'This is what I want. It's my decision, Marion. You can say what you like. It will make no difference. I promised Ray that we'll give it a chance, and I won't go back on what I said.'

Marion paced the footpath. 'I just don't understand this. None of it. Two days ago you were talking about getting a place for yourself. What's changed?'

'Nothing,' Oona said. 'I love him. Maybe I'd forgotten that.'

'Love? Oona, for fuck's sake. You can't love a man who belted you senseless,' Marion said, although she knew, that as crazy as the idea appeared, it was possible. 'Whatever you're feeling it can't be love.'

'But it is. And he didn't belt me senseless. It wasn't as bad as that. I shouldn't have argued with him.'

Marion had had enough. Whatever excuses Oona provided, Marion knew that her sister was lying to herself. 'Do me a favour. The next time he belts you, all I would ask you to do is take a good look at yourself in the mirror.'

'Why would I do that?' Oona asked.

'Because what you'll discover will have fuck-all to do with love. You'll see blood and bruises. Not love.'

Oona sneered at her sister. 'You don't understand, Marion.'

'You're right about that, Oona. I don't understand any of this.'

'Would you like me to tell you why?' Oona suggested, desperate to turn her barely hidden shame against her sister.

'Go ahead.'

'You don't have a man in your life, and you haven't had one for a long time, Marion. Even when you were with Stan, I never heard you say you loved him.'

'You don't know what you're talking about. You were hardly ever around when Stan and me were together,' Marion said.

'I saw enough. And look at you now. I don't want to end up on my own. I need to be with someone. And it's Ray.'

In that moment, as odd as it appeared to her, Marion felt the weight of responsibility for her sister's welfare lift from her body, a sense of relief she would later find difficult to admit to herself. It was clear to her that no pleading, demanding or tears on her part would have an impact on Oona's decision. She would no longer be responsible for the choices her sister made. There was nothing more to say, except what Marion felt she needed to, in her own defence.

'Oona, if you want to risk your life with Ray Lomax, that's up to you. I don't want you to do this to yourself, because I know you're making a terrible mistake. And I love you. But there's nothing I can do to stop it from happening.'

'You're right,' Oona said, a little too smug for Marion's liking.

'Have you thought about how Dad will feel about this?' Marion asked. 'I'll have to tell him. He'll be shattered.'

In a poor attempt to hide the pain of her father's concern, Oona shrugged her shoulders and said nothing.

'I need you to listen to me for a final time,' Marion asked. 'I mean, really listen. Can you at least do that for me?'

'Sure,' Oona said. 'But I need to go soon. Ray will be waiting upstairs for me. He's taking me out for a meal. In the city. To a private club, he says.'

Marion looked her sister in the eye until she felt she had Oona's full attention.

'Good for you. You run upstairs to Ray and let him take you out to dinner at some fancy place. And be sure you enjoy yourself, Oona. And then also be sure that you're ready for the follow-up tomorrow. And the next day. Because it will come at you hard.' She shook a finger in Oona's face. 'And when it falls apart, you're not to come running to me and upsetting the kids. You say that I never liked Ray? It's more than that, Oona. Ray Lomax is a bully and a pig. I fucking hate him.'

'There'll be no need for me to come running to your place. Ever again. You won't be seeing me. And I don't care what you think of Ray.'

'Another thing,' Marion said, ignoring the threat. 'Don't forget this either. Don't you dare give me grief about living on my own. It's what I want for me and my children. I haven't had a man tell me what to do in a long time. And I've never had one knock me around. You make your choices, Oona, and I'll make my own.'

'I've made mine,' Oona said. 'And I'm happy with them. Goodbye.'

Marion stood on the footpath and watched her sister walk away, across the entrance way and up a flight of stairs towards the flat. She couldn't bring herself to turn and leave until Oona was out of sight.

Oona stood at the door into the flat and hesitated, well knowing that if she could not save herself from what lay ahead, at least those she loved would not have to deal with Ray Lomax or the pain that followed one of his outbursts.

Heading back to work through the gardens, Marion already regretted her words to Oona. They may have been true but would've been best left unspoken. She thought about her father, and how she could possibly explain to him that Oona had returned to a monster. Charlie would worry himself sick. There was no point in delaying the news, Marion thought. She'd call by the house and speak with her father after work.

Marion was shocked when Ray Lomax walked into the dry cleaners around a half-hour before closing time. He had several white shirts draped over one arm. Ray laid the shirts out on the counter. 'I'll have these cleaned and pressed,' he said to Marion. The bell above the front door rang behind him, and a second customer came into the shop – a woman carrying a stuffed laundry bag.

'I'll get someone to help you,' Marion said, without looking at Ray. 'I'll take care of the lady.'

'No, you won't,' he said, beating both hands on the countertop, as if he was playing a set of bongos. 'I want you to serve me.' He winked at Marion. 'I was hoping that I might get a family discount.'

Marion noticed the flash of a silver ring with a blood-red ruby in the centre, adorning Ray's right hand. The same ring had broken her sister's face. She felt heat rise through her body. 'Don't think you can come by here and rub it in my nose, Ray. We're not family,' she said. 'Far from it. You can fuck off out of the shop.'

The woman holding the laundry bag frowned.

'Excuse me,' Ray said. 'You can't speak to a customer that way. Swearing at me.' He turned to the woman. 'Did you hear what she just said? I think I'll have words with her boss.'

'Do what you like,' Marion said. 'I don't care. Maybe you should have a word with the police while you're at it and let them know about your own behaviour.'

Ray reached for Marion's arm. She stepped back, too quickly for him to grab hold of her. 'Don't you threaten me,' he said.

'I'm not threatening you, Ray. I'm telling you. I don't want you laying another hand on my sister. That's all I expect from you. It wouldn't be much to ask of a man with any decency.' Marion leaned across the counter. 'You need to know this, Ray. I'll do whatever it takes to save my sister from you.'

He bundled the shirts together and stuck them under his arm. 'Oona told me about the argument you had with her on the street. You upset her so badly, she came into the flat in tears. Wait until she hears about this. She won't want to see you in a hurry.'

'And I don't want to see you,' Marion answered. 'Not see you or hear one word out of your lying mouth.'

Ray whispered, 'Fuck you, bitch,' turned, smiled at the woman standing behind him and left.

A little later Marion closed the shop and walked slowly to her father's house, searching for the courage to explain what Oona had done. She opened the kitchen door without bothering to knock.

Charlie was sitting at the table sorting through a jar of glass marbles. 'You only just missed Joe,' he said. 'He'll be home with Oona by now.'

'He won't be, Dad. Not with Oona,' Marion said. 'She's not at my place any longer.'

Marion relayed the conversation she'd had with her sister and the details of Ray's visit to the shop. Charlie initially said nothing in response. It was as if he hadn't heard a word his daughter said to him. He dug a hand into the jar and collected another marble. He held it to the lightbulb above the table and twirled it between a finger and thumb. He then cleaned and polished the marble with a cloth and placed it in a second jar, among other marbles he'd cleaned. He repeated the process a second and a third time before responding to his daughter.

'Joe will enjoy these,' he said. 'What do you think?'

'I'm sure he will, Dad. He'll love them.'

Charlie held another marble to the light, a larger one. 'We used to call these ones Tom Bowlers. The big boys.' He swivelled the marble between his fingers. 'Look at the light, Marion. It's catching the silver sparkles in the glass. It's magical.'

Marion had always admired her father's ability to discover beauty in simple objects. He kept polishing as he told his daughter a story.

'When I was around twelve years old, I caught the measles. You wouldn't believe how sick I was. I had a temperature through the roof and pounding headaches that went on for days. We were living in two rooms on the top floor of a boarding house. My mother, your nanna, moved a stretcher bed into the room beside my own and slept next to me the whole time I was unwell. I'd wake in the night with a fever and her hand would be in mine. She was on her own by then, with us four kids.'

'Where was your father?'

'Oh, she'd left him by then. She'd had enough and we took off one morning after he left for work. The years of his madness, she couldn't take any more,' Charlie said.

Marion was curious. 'Did he come after her, to get her back?'

'No. I think he was happy to be rid of us. My father was such a selfish man, his own children got in his way just for breathing.'

Marion watched as her father admired the large marble. No-one had ever taught him to be a loving father and she was proud of him for simply being who he was. Although her father's childhood had mostly been a closed subject, Marion risked another question.

'Did you see him again, after running away?'

'Oh, I did,' Charlie said. 'About fifteen years later. I was on the broom by then and word was sent that he'd died. I went to his funeral, just to be sure he was dead.' Charlie dropped the Tom Bowler in the second jar and collected another from the first.

'My mother told me stories when I was ill, with these same marbles.' He held another to the light. 'My brother, Matthew, kept them in a football sock. Mum took one in her hand and explained to me that there was life inside. A world in miniature. All I had to do was look closely and I would see it. Each marble had its own story and its own people. She told me these stories for days. A story for every marble in the collection. You know what I admired about that woman?'

'What?'

'That after all she'd been through with him, the violence, all his belittling talk to break her spirit, she never lost her imagination. She hid it from him, but once she was free, she was able to share it with us. A simple act from my mother. It taught me such a lesson.'

'And what was that?'

'Care.' Charlie smiled. 'It costs nothing.'

Charlie placed the final polished marble in the glass jar and screwed the lid down. He picked up a pen and wrote on the lid of the jar – *the property of Joe Cluny.* He passed the jar to Marion. 'Take this home for Joe. Please.'

'Thank you. I should go,' Marion said. 'Seeing as he's on his own.'

Charlie stood and rested his back against the kitchen sink. He buried his hands in his pants pockets. 'When did it start between Oona and him?' he asked. 'The first time?'

'I can't be sure,' Marion said, speaking as calmly and honestly as she ever had with her father about the violence her sister had been subject to. 'It would have been not long after she moved in with him. They'd only been together for six months, and I begged her to wait a little longer. It was too early, I told her. I was biding my time, hoping she'd get over him, work him out for what he was before it was too late for her. It had been all roses before that. The bastard waited until he'd captured her. Oona never said a word to me, but I knew. Not so much the bruises. She did a reasonable job of hiding them. It was her mood.'

'How so?' Charlie asked. 'I didn't notice any change in her.'

'Sorry to tell you this, Dad. But men never do. She went so quiet. Lost her voice. That front she'd always had as a kid, standing up for herself against anyone who tried bossing her. It was gone.'

Charlie's shoulders collapsed. Marion had never seen her father look so beaten down. 'She's held on to a secret for a long time,' he said. 'I knew nothing.'

'Maybe you did know, Dad? I think we all know. The biggest secrets on these streets are the ones that we share, but somehow find ways to ignore. And to pretend. No matter how often I tried to convince myself there was nothing bad going on between Oona and Ray, all along I knew I was lying to myself. I think we always know, Dad.'

ELEVEN

Ruby was on her way home. Marion and Joe went into the city on the tram to meet her at the railway station. They arrived early and headed to the cafeteria, where Joe ordered a fifty-fifty cordial and a meat pie with sauce. Marion looked at the menu on a large board behind the counter and asked for the exotically named 'Americano Coffee'. She struggled to distract herself with thoughts of Oona but was glad that Ruby was returning. Her daughter's spirit always managed to lift Marion's own.

'You must be pleased that your sister will be home?' she said.

Although Joe was excited about Ruby's return, he preferred not to admit it and didn't reply. He dug a fork into the top of his pie, considering a question of his own that he'd thought about during the tram ride. He ate several mouthfuls of the pie before asking, 'Are we going to tell Ruby about Aunty Oona?'

'What do we need to tell her?' Marion asked, evasively.

'That she came to stay,' Joe said.

'There's not much excitement in telling Ruby that her aunty was over. But maybe it's best to tell her once she's settled back in. You know how much Ruby loves Oona. She'll be jealous that you had her all to yourself.'

'I might be jealous that I didn't have a holiday away,' Joe said.

'I don't think so. You were lucky to enjoy spending time with your grandfather,' Marion said. 'Ruby missed out on that also.'

'I was lucky,' Joe agreed. 'Char said I can come next week, even though Ruby is back. We have more jobs to finish. I'll go to the pool one day with Ruby and then have another with Char.'

He ate the remains of his pie as he worked up the courage to say what had been on his mind since his aunty had left the house. 'I liked Oona being with us. It would be better if she'd stayed,' he said.

Better, Marion thought. A simple and yet loaded word. She raked a hand through Joe's unruly hair. 'It might have been better. But Oona wanted to go home to her own place. It was her decision,' Marion added, as if pre-empting a looming disaster.

Joe was missing the nightly stories told in bed. As well as the tale about Lena, the girl who ran away to the circus, Oona knew many other stories that had not been written in books. 'Where did you learn all of them?' he asked her one night.

'The story of Lena and the circus, from your grandfather. Some he made up himself, and others he'd heard from his mother and grandmother.'

'How do you remember so many stories?' Joe had asked.

'I'm not sure,' Oona had replied. She'd seemed surprised herself that she was easily able to recall stories that her father had told her when she was a child. Some that she hadn't heard for many years. 'I just do. And now it's your turn to remember, Joe.'

'Did Char ever tell you about the talking dog?' he asked.

'He sure did. We all have to know the story of the talking dog and what happened to him. That's a very important story.'

Joe had also enjoyed sitting in the kitchen listening to his mother and aunty singing together and dancing around the room. His feelings of happiness towards them both would sometimes become clouded by the images of Oona's body he'd seen on the first night she was at the house. While Marion avoided all talk about Oona's bruises, his grandfather's explosion of anger in the kitchen was enough for Joe to realise that it was Ray Lomax who'd hurt her. When his mother told him that she'd left and returned to Ray, Joe thought about the line in the 'Jack and Jill' nursery rhyme. Unlike Jack, whose body had been repaired with 'vinegar and brown paper', his mother and grandfather, between them, hadn't been able to put Oona back together again.

As she sat and drank her coffee Marion listened for the arrival announcements. 'We need to go,' she said. 'Ruby's train is in.'

Standing on the platform, Joe could see the train in the distance, rounding a bend. A diesel engine drawing ten silver carriages. The longest train he'd ever seen soon pulled into the platform, its engine spewing fumes. People stepped down from the carriages carrying suitcases, boxes, pets in cages, wheeling bicycles and nursing sleeping babies. Joe caught a glimpse of Ruby in the crowd although, at first, he wasn't sure he was looking at his sister. Ruby had changed so much in a short space of time. Her skin had browned, and her cheeks and nose were freckled. And she seemed so much older.

Marion noticed a change in her daughter also and was a little shocked. Looking at Ruby standing on the platform, swinging her case at her side, Marion saw Oona as much as she did her daughter. People often commented that they looked alike, but the stark recognition of a deeper resemblance between the pair left Marion feeling uneasy.

Spotting her mother, Ruby ran to her and hugged Marion, who kissed her daughter. 'Look at you. God. You look so healthy, Ruby. Farm life has done you good. Have you missed us?'

'I have,' Ruby said. 'I had a wonderful holiday. But I did miss you, Mum.' She smiled at Joe. 'And even him. Now and then. Did you miss me, Joe?'

'Not too much,' Joe said, admiring the colour in his sister's cheeks. 'I've been busy working with Char, sorting through his collection.'

'Anything exciting happen while I've been away?' Ruby asked, walking beside her mother down the ramp and into the bowels of the station. Neither Joe nor Marion was certain of how to best answer the question.

'Let's get home,' Marion said. 'We'll eat out at the cafe tonight. Would you like that, Ruby?'

'Yes, Mum. I'd love that.'

★

The temperature the following day was expected to reach the century and Ruby and Joe went to the pool in the gardens. They made their own lunch and packed it in a canvas bag with a bottle of cordial.

When they arrived, the surrounding grassed areas were already busy. Ruby found a spot in the shade under a weeping willow and laid out their towels, staking their claim for the day. A group of girls from Ruby's school year were sitting nearby. She went and joined them, excited to talk about her holiday.

Joe went into the water alone. The pool was due to be emptied and cleaned the following morning. The water was murky and the concrete bottom, coated in slime, was slippery. Joe soon joined in a game with some other boys. Standing at the shallow edge, each boy would run into the water and use the soles of their feet to slide across the base of the pool for as long as possible until collapsing into the water.

After the game Joe returned to the tree, exhausted. His and Ruby's towels had been thrown against a hedge along with their lunch bag. A group of older boys had taken their place under the shade. Joe collected the towels, slung the canvas bag over his shoulder and walked down to the edge of the pool.

Ruby saw him and waded from the water. 'What are you doing, Joe? We had a good spot out of the sun.

You shouldn't have moved our things. We'll lose our place now.'

'I didn't move anything,' he said. 'Some boys took our place.'

'Took it?' she said. 'It can't be taken. It's ours. That's the rule here and everybody knows it.'

Joe didn't feel that the boys would care at all about any rules, particularly those that had not been written down.

'Well, they took it. And they threw our towels away,' Joe said. 'I'll find another place for us.'

'No, you won't. We already have our place and I'm going to take it back.'

'But they're boys,' Joe said. 'And there's three of them.'

'I don't care who they are. Or how many. No boys can take our place away from us.'

Ruby walked across the grass, dodging sunburnt bodies. Two of the boys were sitting up, sharing a cigarette. A third was lying on his back, a white t-shirt covering his face.

Ruby stood over the seated pair. 'Hey,' she said. The boys ignored her. 'Hey,' she repeated, more loudly. 'We were here first. You need to move away.'

They laughed and ignored her request. Ruby persisted. 'We were here before you,' she repeated. 'My brother and me. We had our towels laid out right here. That's the rule. You will have to move to someplace else.'

One of the boys, pimple-faced with a Beatles fringe hiding his eyes, took a drag on the cigarette. 'The grass doesn't belong to you, and there are no rules here. Go find somewhere else for you and your brother.' He looked up at Joe, pointed to his birthmark and laughed. 'It looks like someone has rubbed shit on your face, kid. You should go down to the water and clean it off.'

'Don't speak about my brother like that,' Ruby said. 'You're only able to sit here because you threw our towels and bag away.' She folded her arms across her chest. 'I need you to leave. Now.'

'Are you deaf?' the boy said. 'Your brother's got crap on his face and you can't hear a word. What a fucking pair. Do you need me to shout it out for you? We're not moving.' He spat on the grass, close by Ruby's feet. 'Piss off.'

'That's your answer?' Ruby asked.

'Yep. That's my answer.'

'Well, thank you,' Ruby said.

She walked back down to the edge of the pool. Joe didn't want trouble with the boys and was relieved that Ruby had given up on her demand. Ruby spoke with a young girl at the side of the pool, who was playing with a plastic bucket. The girl handed the bucket to Ruby and she filled it. She marched back across the grass, stopped in front of the three boys and poured the bucket of water over the head of the boy who'd sworn at her.

He jumped to his feet and stuck his face in Ruby's. 'What the fuck are you doing?'

'I asked you nicely for our spot. We want it back. That's what I'm doing,' she said. 'And don't you swear at me.'

The boy thumped Ruby in the chest, hard enough that she fell backwards, over the top of another girl, onto the grass. Joe didn't know what to do. The boy was bigger and older than he was, and Joe was afraid. He ran to help Ruby.

She sat up and Joe offered his hand. 'Thank you,' she said.

Ruby got to her feet and charged at the boy, throwing her body against his, her fists slamming into his face. They tumbled to the ground and Ruby landed on top of him. She dug her knees into his chest. He had a bloodied nose and struggled to move under the weight of her body.

'You took our place,' Ruby shouted, holding a clenched fist in the boy's face. 'And now we're taking it back. You and your friends will have to find somewhere else to sit. Do you understand me?'

The boy squirmed under the weight of Ruby's body. 'Get off me,' he screamed. A crowd of children gathered around them.

'Do you understand me?' she repeated.

'Yes,' he said. 'Get off me.'

She climbed off the boy. He rolled over, stood up, retreated with his friends and called out, 'Fucking bitch.'

Joe had never felt prouder of his sister. He couldn't take his eyes off her.

'What?' she said, nonchalantly, as if what she'd just done was nothing out of the ordinary for a thirteen-year-old girl confronting a bullying boy.

'Nothing,' he said, aware that the scene he'd just witnessed meant everything to him.

They sat and shared lunch together. The previous night, when they ate out at the cafe, Marion had briefly mentioned that Oona had been staying with them, but said little more, avoiding all questions from her daughter. Ruby suspected that there was more to tell.

She finished her sandwich and folded her towel. 'Why did Oona stay over?' she asked, as casually as she could manage.

'I don't know,' Joe answered. 'She just stayed.'

'Why would she do that?' Ruby pointed in the

direction of Oona's flat, across the other side of the park. 'She lives just there. It's not like the holiday that I had. Hundreds of miles away. She's never stayed with us before.'

'I told you, I don't know,' Joe said, his face becoming flushed. 'She just did.'

Ruby was certain that her brother was lying and that her mother was keeping something from her. She was determined to find out why they were being so secretive.

During the walk home, Ruby told Joe stories about her holiday. 'Learning to ride the pushbike was the hardest of all,' she said. 'At first, anyway. One of the girls who lives on the farm, Vanessa, she held the bike steady for me. I hopped onto a bucket that had been turned upside down, got on and pedalled as fast as I could. She ran alongside the bike, keeping it steady and screaming out "pedal, pedal" until I was able to hold my balance. It took me a full day to learn to ride on my own.'

'What about the canoeing you wrote about on the postcard?' Joe asked.

'I loved the canoes too. The family had a dam out the back of the house. The parents were working on the farm during the day and left us to do whatever we wanted. The water in the dam was deep and dark, and we swam every afternoon. Learning to steer the canoe through the water was easier than riding the bike. Once I got used to both, I went from the canoe to the bike and back again. All day.'

'I think I would like a holiday next year,' he said. 'Do you think I could go to the same farm?'

'Maybe. But first, you'll have to learn to behave yourself at school. Then you might get lucky and have a turn.'

'Did you learn anything else?' he asked.

'I did,' Ruby said. 'I learned to fight. Vanessa is a year older than me. And her younger sister, Kate, is the same age as you. They can both fight, as good as any boy. Or better. They get into fights all the time.'

'Who do they fight with?' Joe asked.

'Their brothers if no-one else is around. But mostly the boys from the farm next door. They're twins, and the same age as me. The second day I was at the farm we were swimming in the dam and one of them threw a handful of mud at Kate. It got her in the eye, and she couldn't see out of it. When Vanessa yelled at them to stop, the other twin threw a stone at her. It hit Vanessa on the cheek and cut her skin.'

'What did she do?'

'She swam after the boy and dragged him out of the

dam. And she challenged him to a fight.'

Joe thought about Ruby charging at the boy at the swimming pool. 'Did she fight with her fists like you just did?'

'Yep. She belted him in the head until he cried. And then she shoved a handful of mud in his mouth. She almost choked him to death.'

'Mud?'

'Yep. Mud. Vanessa also showed me how to kick a boy in the balls and hurt him. She's crippled both of her brothers doing that.'

'The balls.' Joe laughed out loud hearing his sister use the word. 'Balls,' he repeated.

'Yep, Joe. Balls. They are a boy's weak spot. Vanessa taught me that. She taught me other stuff as well.'

Although she was less than two years older than him, for the first time in his life, Joe looked at Ruby and realised that one day she would be a woman. The thought worried him. He didn't want to lose his sister.

They turned into their street. 'Wait up,' Ruby said. 'Before we go inside, I know there's more to tell about Oona. I need to know, Joe.'

'There's nothing to tell,' he said. 'She came while you were away. That's all. She slept in your bed and told me stories. The rest of the time she watched TV.'

'Last night, when we were eating, I asked Mum

about why Oona had come over and she wouldn't tell me. Why would Mum do that? You're both lying to me, Joe. Tell me what happened when I was away.'

Joe was saved from Ruby's interrogation by their mother. She was standing on the footpath outside the house, waiting for them to come inside.

'Don't you say a word about my fight with the boy,' Ruby whispered to Joe, 'or I'll have to kill you.'

'I won't.'

'And nothing about balls either.'

'No balls,' he whispered.

'What did you get up to at the pool?' Marion asked.

Ruby was quick with an answer. 'We swam and ate our sandwiches and then we had another swim. And I met some girls from school.'

'I suppose I won't need to feed you then,' Marion said. 'The kitchen's a furnace with this heat. Come and sit in the yard. I have something to tell you both.'

They sat while Marion fetched three glasses of iced water then joined her children under the only shade available, an old apple tree. She waited until they'd each had a drink before breaking the news to them.

'After the words I had with the priest last week, I made enquiries about a new school for you, Joe. This year is your first in high school, and if we're going to make a change, now is the time to do it. The state high school by the river has a new building and classes begin there in a few weeks.'

'Mum, what words did you have with the priest?' Ruby asked.

'Never mind,' Marion replied. 'This is about Joe changing schools.'

Joe couldn't hide his smile at the thought of escaping the nuns. He put a hand in the air, as if he was in class.

'Yes?' Marion said.

'I have two questions,' he said.

'Well, ask them. And there's no need to put your hand up.'

'Do they have the strap at the high school?' he asked.

'Well, yes and no,' she said. 'I spoke to the headmaster, and he told me they have options for students.'

'Like what?

'If a student gets in serious trouble at school, they can choose either the strap or detention. It's up to the student to decide. Those are the options.'

Before Joe could ask what detention referred to, Ruby explained the concept to him. 'Detention means that you're kept back after school with all the other troublemakers, and you must do extra classwork. You'll be spending plenty of time in detention, Joe. I wouldn't be surprised if they name it after you. *Joe Time.*'

Thinking about the television programs he could miss out on of an afternoon, Joe wanted more information. 'How long does detention go for?'

'You don't need to know that,' his mother said. 'I need to see change in you, Joe. And I've decided you won't be getting into trouble at school. There will be no nuns for you to aggravate every day of the week. If you did happen to get into trouble at the high school,' she added, 'you wouldn't have to worry about detention because I'll send you straight back to Sister Mary Josephine.'

'Mum?' Ruby said. 'When did you decide to change Joe's school? Nobody asked me about this.'

'I haven't had the time to tell you. This needs to happen. I need Joe to try something new, away from Our Lady's.'

The idea of leaving the nuns appealed to Ruby also. She'd had enough of disguising herself as one of God's angels. 'I'll have to go with him,' she said. 'You can't send Joe there on his own. He'll get slaughtered. Boys from the state school are rough.'

'That won't be happening,' Marion said. 'You're one of the best students at Our Lady's.'

'Please let me go with him,' Ruby pleaded. 'If it doesn't work out, I can always go back. I'll still be top of the class at the high school. State kids are not as smart as us. Half of them can't read or write.' She smiled at Joe. 'Even you could be dux in class.'

Joe doubted he'd ever be dux of anything. 'I'd like Ruby to come with me,' he said to his mother. 'Please.'

'Thank you,' Ruby mouthed when her mother wasn't looking.

'I'm not sure about this,' Marion said. 'I'll need time to think this over. For now, Ruby, you'll be staying where you are.'

TWELVE

CHARLIE WAS OUT OF BED early the following morning and had filled the wagon with brass taps, more copper pipe and a cast-iron sink before Joe arrived for the day. He was sitting at the table inspecting the fully restored revolver when Joe came into the kitchen. 'I'm giving this a final clean before the sale,' Charlie explained.

Joe sat down and looked at the revolver. 'Have you ever fired a gun?' he asked.

'Never. I hadn't held one in my hand until you found this.'

'Will it work properly now that you've fixed it?' Joe asked.

'According to Ranji it will. He's certain we'll get good money for it. I've loaded the last of the scrap into the wagon. Let's see if he's found a buyer for us.'

Charlie wrapped the gun in a cloth and put it into his satchel and they set off to visit Ranji.

At the scrapyard Ranji was busy freeing the corpse of a rat from a trap he'd set the night before. A colony of rats lived in a drainage pipe that lay beside the canal that bordered the gasworks. Ranji held the dead rodent by its tail, which was at least a foot long, as was its bloodied carcass. 'Take a look at this one,' he said to Joe. 'His head has been near taken off by the trap.'

Joe was afraid of rats. Dead or alive. 'No, thank you,' he said, refusing to look at the near decapitated animal.

'Don't be frightened by him,' Ranji said. 'This one is as dead as Ned Kelly. The rats around here are a breed like no other. I hear there is an old woman getting around the lanes poisoning the rats with arsenic and milk. I need to get her down here.'

'I know her,' Joe said, recalling the story circulating in the schoolyard about the old woman who cleaned the milk bottles. 'I thought it was cats she was killing.'

'No, it is certainly rats. If you see her, Joe, please let the woman know I have employment for her. It will be some task. It is believed that this species are the largest rats in the state, if not the country,' Ranji added.

'Where'd you hear that?' Charlie asked, doubting Ranji's story.

'That information came direct from the mouth of a university man,' Ranji said. 'The man is a professor.'

'What sort of professor was he?'

'The educated sort, you imbecile. I just told you. A university man. He came by my yard some time back and we had a serious discussion about the rats. The same professor was bitten by one of the same breed of rats during his research. Subsequently, his head swelled like a balloon, and he hasn't been able to speak a word since. The man has a form of lockjaw.'

'*Subsequently*, my arse,' Charlie said.

Although Joe didn't want to show disrespect to Ranji, he couldn't help but laugh, which encouraged his grandfather to continue the niggle.

'For your information, lockjaw is an affliction caused by being bitten by rabid dogs, not rats. I saw it in that movie, the one where Gregory Peck shoots the crazed dog. There is a difference, Ranji, between a dog and a rat.'

'*Affliction*,' Ranji scoffed. He turned to Joe. 'Listen to your poor grandfather. He is trying to outdo me with a fancy word that I guarantee he cannot spell. You watch me, Joe, and I'll show you something to interest you. An experiment.'

Ranji laid the dead rat on the ground, went over to one of the forty-fours and fished around until he'd found a length of wire. He picked the rat up and wound the wire around its carcass. 'Follow me,' he said.

Ranji headed across to the acid bath, with Joe pacing behind at a safe distance. Ranji dropped the rat into the tank and secured the end of the piece of wire to a metal bar running the length of the tank. 'We'll come back later on and check on him.'

Charlie hunted around in his pocket and brought out a shilling coin. 'I've got business to talk over with Ranji,' he said to Joe. 'I'll leave you to unload the wagon. Except for the sink, of course.' He handed the coin to Joe. 'Here's your wages. In advance. Add it to your moneybox.'

Ranji had positive news about the revolver. He'd found a buyer, after a visit to a dealer on the other side of the river. He told Charlie that the walls of the gun shop were lined with the mounted heads of animals that had been shot, skinned and stuffed. Mostly deer and wild pigs.

'The man brought out a book from beneath the counter. On each page there were photographs and details of many different guns and pistols. I recognised ours, and the dealer whistled loudly.'

The shop owner then contacted a collector on Ranji's behalf and provided him with the details of the make and model of the handgun. The collector immediately made an offer.

'The shop owner said to me that if the revolver is in good order, that being what you and I, Charlie, understand as perfect working order, then the collector is willing to pay sixty pounds. Sixty,' Ranji repeated. 'That is a very good earn, my friend.'

'Sixty pounds split three ways is twenty each for me and you, and another twenty for Joe. That will be a fortune for him.' Charlie took the pistol out of his satchel, unwrapped it and held it in his hand. 'Is sixty enough, do you think? Maybe if we hold off and ask around some more, we might get a better offer.'

Ranji was quick to disagree. 'My friend. You are an amateur in the world of enterprise. Let me give you the advice of an experienced businessman. Sixty in the hand is money guaranteed. We could wait for a better offer, but we may not get it. If we try a game of bluff with this man, we may lose him. He is a fish on the line, and he is taking a big bite. I've been in the trade for many years, and I am known as Ranji Khan the businessman, not Ranji the hopeless gambler. And remember this: if your grandson had not found the pistol in the wooden chest, we would not have sixty pounds. We would have nothing. I say we take the money.'

'You know best,' Charlie said. 'Let's celebrate with a cup of tea.'

'And a biscuit,' Ranji said. He pulled a watch out of his pocket and checked the time. 'And when the tea is over, I will go and pray.'

When Ranji returned to the shed with his hessian mat, Charlie had a question for him. 'Ever since I've known you, Ranji, you've prayed each day. I've never known you to miss. Have you always prayed?'

Ranji smiled. 'You are asking me such a question after so many years? I'm surprised, Charlie. Why ask me now?'

'I'm just curious,' Charlie said.

'And you were never curious before now?'

'I've always been interested,' Charlie said. 'I just didn't think to ask you until now.'

Charlie may not have realised it himself, but his interest in Ranji's dedication to prayer had been prompted by his grandson's curiosity about religion.

Ranji sat back in his chair and considered his answer before he spoke.

'I can tell you that I never prayed as a child. Or when I was a younger man,' he added. 'And I had never seen my father pray. If questions of religion came up around our family table, or we heard such a story on the radio we sat around in the evenings, my father would quickly change the subject. Or turn the radio off. He did not speak a word about faith.'

'But you were a Muslim family?' Charlie asked.

'Barely so. My father wore the headdress, as I do now. It meant nothing to me when I was a boy, to see him with the turban. I thought he was wearing a costume, like the genie in Aladdin's lamp. To my shame now, I was embarrassed by my father, to be seen in his company.'

Ranji paused. He appeared distressed.

'You don't have to say any more,' Charlie said. 'I'm sorry for intruding. I understand what it means to be embarrassed by a father.'

'There is no need to apologise. This is something I would like to tell you. My own father. You know that I once betrayed him when I was a boy?'

'How could you have done that?' Charlie asked. He was sceptical that his good-natured and generous friend could ever betray any person, let alone a parent.

'I used to help him with his cart on weekends. He worked six days of every week, selling threads, cloth and needles. My father was a haberdashery man, as they call the business in this country. A cowbell was attached to his cart and when we entered a street I would ring the bell and the women would open their doors and come and buy from him. One day, when we were selling, several teenage boys attacked my father with rocks.

'They screamed at him and called him names. *Dago. Nigger. Abdul the Camel Man.* Other names. He ignored them and continued pushing the cart, even when a stone hit him in the head and drew blood. When I saw the blood on his face I ran away, fearful for myself, with no concern for him. I left my father alone on the street, knowing he would do nothing to protect himself. I thought he must have been afraid of them. A grown man confronted by schoolboys. In my mind he was a coward.'

'What should he have done?' Charlie asked.

'I wanted my father to beat them. To hurt them. I wanted to see fear in the faces of those pale-skinned boys. I wanted him to draw blood from their bodies.'

Charlie had listened carefully to the story. He spoke quietly to his friend. 'You didn't betray him. You were only a kid, and you were frightened. I would have run away too.'

'I don't believe you would have run,' Ranji said. 'You are stronger than me, Charlie. You would have stood up to those boys.'

'No, Ranji. I would have run away. And very quickly,' Charlie insisted.

'What happened that day, it showed that I knew little about my father, throughout his life,' Ranji said. 'I never really understood him. Only after his death did I come to know him as a man.'

'What did you learn about him?' Charlie asked.

'All of his life, my father worked on the cart. That was all I knew about him for all our time together. He died after a heart attack on the street, while pushing a cartload of goods. My mother arranged for his funeral to be held only two days after his death. "Why are we in such a hurry?" I asked her at the time. She would say nothing more than, "It is the way." Her words were a mystery to me. I had no idea what she was talking about.

'When I arrived at the funeral service, I saw my father, not in a wooden coffin as I had expected, but wrapped in a plain shroud. A white colour. His body was surrounded by a group of men I had not seen before. They prepared his body for the next world. They were praying over my father's body. My mother sat alone on a straight-backed wooden chair away from the body and did not speak a word.'

'Did you pray for him yourself?' Charlie asked.

'Not at the time, I didn't know how to pray. I was puzzled about the men who attended to his body. It had such an impact on me. Afterwards, in my mother's house, I questioned her about the service and the men. "Why were there prayers for my father when he was not a religious man," I asked her. She did not reply, which didn't surprise me. Whenever my mother wanted to refuse a question, she always complained of the deafness she did not suffer from. She learned to do this soon after they arrived in this country. She stood up, went into the bedroom and returned with a large envelope. It was worn and creased, with a government seal on the back. She opened the envelope and allowed the contents to spill onto the table.'

Ranji took a handkerchief from his pocket, wiped his forehead and took a sip of tea. 'I am sorry to bore you. You don't need to know any more of this. It is not an important story for you.'

'But it is,' Charlie said. 'Please finish.'

Ranji drained the remains of his teacup.

'It was a government file. From the Immigration Department. Documents, letters and photographs of my father. Front-on photographs, side profile, and even his finger and palm prints. It was as if my father was a criminal. But he was no criminal. He never had been. As one of the letters stated, from a man he did business with, apparently my father was *as good as a white man*.'

Ranji appeared disgusted by the words he'd spoken.

'As good as a white man. What sort of rubbish is

that? That is why my father never prayed. Or taught his children about faith. He wanted us to be accepted in this country. To do so required him to behave like a white man. But those on the street, the people he did business with, knew he was no white man at all. All my life with him, when I was a child, my father looked at the ground and not the sky. I despised that behaviour in him most of all. And I blamed him.'

To escape the thoughts eating at him, Ranji jumped up from his chair and went to the door of the shed, as if he was searching for the boys who'd attacked his father all those years ago.

'That same night, after he had been cremated, I sat and read his file several times. I could not sleep. The next morning, I looked at my own face in the shaving mirror. My brown face. The face of a Khan. A Muslim. I asked my mother about the people who had prepared his body and I went to see them at the mosque, which was nothing more than an iron shed in the yard behind a narrow house. I was given a copy of the Koran and the next day I began to pray.'

'And you believe in your God? The one you pray to?'

'I cannot answer the question,' Ranji said.

'I shouldn't have asked,' Charlie said. 'I'm sorry. It's personal. I understand that myself.'

'Don't be sorry. The reason I cannot answer is

because I still have no idea if there is a God. I don't think about a question of belief. All I do know is that I find peace when I pray. Most of all, I know I am close to my father, and that is more than enough for me. And this is enough old-man talk between the two of us. We are working men, not university professors. So, Charlie, do we accept the deal on the revolver?'

'We do,' Charlie said.

'Good. I need to go and check on my rat.'

Joe had been busy rolling a motorcycle tyre from one end of the yard to the other. He was covered in dust from head to toe. Ranji invited him over to the tank. Joe stood and watched while Ranji unhooked the wire from the metal bar. He lifted the dead rat out of the acid bath. Although it had only been submerged for a short time the fur had been stripped from its body. The flesh, grey in sections and bloodied in others, was covered in blisters. The rodent's head was missing.

As Ranji lowered the body of the rat into the liquid one of its back legs fell away. He looked at his watch. 'If we come back in one hour,' he calculated, 'Mr Rat will be no longer.'

'Today is my Ada's birthday,' Charlie announced after he and Joe had left the scrapyard. He stopped the wagon at a florist shop by the gardens and drove to the cemetery where Ada was buried. It was the oldest graveyard in the city and contained the remains of many thousands of people. Charlie drove through the ornate gates and parked the wagon. 'Let's go pay visit to your nanna.'

Joe followed him along a narrow lane between rows of graves. Some were decorated with headstones, imposing statues and crucifixes. Others lay in ruin, their marble slabs shattered and collapsing into dark and cold hollows. Joe looked over the expanse of the cemetery and couldn't imagine how so many people would fit into Heaven. Or Hell.

They arrived at Ada's grave and Charlie placed the flowers at the foot of the headstone. Joe had occasionally visited with his mother and sister and had read the inscription on his grandmother's headstone. It puzzled him that although the year of her birth was inscribed, there was no day or month recorded on Ada's grave although there was on the headstones surrounding hers. Joe never asked his mother why but, seeing as it was Ada's birthday, Joe had a question for his grandfather.

'How do you know that it's Nanna's birthday?' he asked. 'It isn't written down on the stone.'

'You're right,' Charlie said. 'Your grandmother

didn't know what date she was born, which was terrible for her when she was young. She never had a real celebration for her birthday until she decided to choose today's date to have a party. That didn't happen until after we were married.'

'Why did she pick today?' Joe asked.

'No particular reason except that she said the sun shines more this time of year and she wanted to celebrate her birthday when the weather was good.'

Joe couldn't understand how a person could not have a birthdate, and asked Charlie why it was so for his grandmother.

'Well,' Charlie said, 'we almost never spoke about this when your grandmother was alive. She had no idea of her birthdate because she was an orphan. She had no parents to tell her when she was born. Or a birth certificate with the date. Even the year of her birth was something of guesswork. Your nanna remembered the year she started school and backtracked five years.'

'An orphan?' Joe said. 'How did her mum and dad die?'

They walked along a wide avenue lined with the magnificent marble gravestones in the Italian section of the cemetery. Charlie took Joe's hand.

'Ada never believed that they did die. She once told me that when she was a young woman, she could feel them around her and was convinced they were still alive. She grew up in a religious home. Most of the kids had been taken away from their parents when they were babies.'

'Why would anyone do that?'

'Your parents don't have to be dead to make you an orphan. Even today. Your parents might be poor. Or they were the wrong colour. Like your moneybox friend in the classroom.'

Joe touched his marked cheek. 'Why was Nanna taken away?'

Charlie pictured Ada standing on the front verandah of their house on a Sunday morning, wearing the white dress she preferred for church. Her radiant dark curls and the olive skin, now inherited by her younger daughter, Oona, and granddaughter, Ruby. 'I'm not sure why she was taken,' Charlie said. 'She never knew why. What I do know is that it was a cruel act, what they did to her.'

That evening, after he had eaten tea, Charlie felt restless and decided to go for a walk into the city. It was a warm night and there were many people on the street – families enjoying the air. He strolled by the city's major department store and thought back to a time, so many years earlier, when his mother would gather her children together and tell them they were going 'window shopping'. An activity for people who could never afford to buy the items on display behind the heavy glass. As a child Charlie would put a hand to the window, a teasing distance from the treasures that would never be his own. The trips to the city most often occurred on the nights when their father was at home railing against the world. The family sometimes walked the streets for hours, only daring to return home when their father had exhausted himself and fallen asleep.

Charlie heard a church bell ringing and headed in the direction of the sound until he was standing at the gates of the city cathedral where he'd once sung as a boy. The door was open. Charlie stepped inside, ignored the bowl of holy water. He stood watching a young priest at the front of the cavernous building, preparing the altar for early mass the following morning. He walked along the aisle, stopped and looked up at the gold stars resting on a deep-blue background painted into the ceiling panels high above the altar. They appeared as magical as they had when he first saw them as a child.

'They're beautiful,' the priest said.

'They are,' Charlie answered. 'I remember being

told there is no ceiling like this one in any other church across the city.'

'And most likely no other church in the state. Even for us Catholics, they're a little dazzling.'

'How did they get there?' Charlie asked.

The priest sat at a pew on the side of the altar. 'The story I've been told was that the priest here, when the church was being built, ordered that the stars be painted into the ceiling. When he was later confronted by the archbishop and asked to explain the reason behind the decoration, he answered that he wanted to encourage children to look up and contemplate Heaven, and that he wanted them to see something beautiful.'

'That's wonderful,' Charlie said. 'Such a beautiful story.' Thinking of the persistent questions that Joe had been asking of him lately, he then said, 'And what about Hell? I see that he had nothing painted on the floorboards.'

'I've thought about that myself,' the priest said. 'I expect he was an optimist.' He stood and asked, 'Would you like to pray?'

'No. Not me, Father. It's been too long. I'm well past praying.' Turning to leave, he changed his mind and stopped. 'Could you do so on my behalf? I have a daughter who is in trouble, and I'm worried for her. Do you have time to say a prayer for her?'

'I don't believe that any of us is ever past praying,' the priest said. 'But of course. I can pray for her. What is your daughter's name?'

'Oona,' Charlie said. 'Oona Cluny. Thank you, Father.'

Charlie left the church and began walking home just as the weather turned. A clap of thunder was quickly followed by heavy rain, falling in large drops. Charlie didn't bother seeking cover and his clothing was soon drenched through. He looked into the dark sky and felt soothed by the raindrops falling on his skin. The visit to the cathedral and the short conversation with the priest had calmed him.

He walked on until he reached the council playground near home. He stopped beside the set of swings where he'd first taken Marion to play when she was a small child, followed some years later by Oona and, in turn, his grandchildren, Ruby and Joe. Charlie rested a hand against the swing, pushed it, stood back, and watched it arc through the night air.

He thought about Oona, and how resilient she'd been as a child. Charlie had never known her to cry. If she had done so, she'd managed to keep her tears from him and Ada both. When she was around five or six years old – Charlie couldn't remember exactly when – he'd collected Oona after school and brought her to the playground. She was playing on the monkey bars, attempting to swing from one end to the other, when she fell and landed on the cold ground below. One side of Oona's face was covered in dirt, and she had a cut on one elbow and grazes on both hands, embedded with grit. She got to her feet, brushed the dirt from her dress and face, climbed straight back onto the play equipment.

Charlie sat on the swing. He looked around to check if there was anyone watching him. He moved backwards, as he remembered doing as a child. He then thrust his body forward, straightened his legs and lifted them into the air. Charlie swung back and forward until the swing slowed and finally stopped. He hopped off and crossed to the spot where Oona had fallen many years earlier.

'You are so brave,' he whispered. The same words he'd used on the afternoon of the fall.

'I am very brave,' he heard Oona answer.

THIRTEEN

RUBY WAS GETTING READY FOR bed when she discovered the metal moneybox Joe had taken from school. Searching in the wardrobe for the pair of gym boots she'd need the next morning, she saw the black-faced boy looking up at her from his hiding place behind a leather football. Ruby took the moneybox out of the wardrobe and shook it, checking if there was money inside. It was empty. Joe had most likely taken the coins and spent them, she expected. Ruby sat the boy on the shelf beside the headless statuette of Jesus Christ, who she had been unable to part with despite his horrific injuries. Ruby then lay on top of her bed and waited on Joe for an explanation.

When he came in, Joe saw the boy looking at him from across the room. The expression on his face as guilty as Joe's own. He ran and snatched the moneybox boy from the shelf. 'He doesn't belong to you,' he said.

Ruby sat up. 'You're right, Joe. He doesn't belong to me. And guess what? He doesn't belong to you either. The moneybox belongs to the school. To the Sisters. You've stolen the money from his stomach that is used to buy food for the starving children who live on the missions.'

'I didn't steal any money,' Joe said.

'Of course you did. I've checked and his stomach is empty.'

'I know it's empty, because I took the coins out and left them on the Sister's desk on the last day of school. I brought the boy home with me. Not the money. I saved him.'

'Saved him from what? Why would you bring the moneybox home?' she asked.

'Because he was sitting on the desk and looking lonely. I didn't want him to be left at the school on his own all summer. He looked at me like he wanted to come with me. If he could speak, I know he would have asked me. So, I picked him up and brought him home.'

'That's the reason? Because he looked at you? He will have to go back to the school.'

Ruby glanced at the moneybox boy. He did appear

to be looking pleadingly at her.

'Not only that,' Joe said. 'I was still angry that Sister Mary Josephine stuck my head in the bucket. She said my face was *filthy*.' Joe put a hand to his dark birthmark. 'Like this is filthy. And the boy too,' he added. 'He is teased because he is dirty. I've heard them say so. Boys in my class.' Joe laid the moneybox on his bed. 'I didn't want to leave him.'

Ruby felt guilty for the many times she'd teased Joe about his birthmark. 'You are plenty of trouble, Joe,' she said. 'But you've never been filthy.'

If Joe was caught for having stolen the moneybox he'd be in serious trouble. From the school, the priest and their mother. It would be the one crime that would see him expelled.

'If you don't go back to Our Lady's this year, how will the boy be returned to the classroom?'

'He's not going back,' Joe said. 'I'm going to keep him.'

'And what if you're caught with him?'

'But I won't be caught. Unless you tell on me, Ruby.'

'Don't worry. I won't be telling on you,' she said. 'You're not ready for Hell.'

Joe dived into the wardrobe and retrieved a second moneybox, the one that Charlie had given him in the shape of the office building.

'There's money in this one,' he said, and shook it. The coins that Joe had been paid for helping his grandfather rattled around inside. 'There's also paper money in here,' Joe explained. 'You can't hear it, but I have a five-pound note.'

'I know where you would have got that,' Ruby said. 'From our father.'

'He said it's for you and me and Mum. Charlie bought me the moneybox and put the five-pound note inside.'

'You're not supposed to take money from him. Mum will be angry if she finds out.'

'I'll only be in trouble if you tell,' Joe repeated.

'Don't worry, I won't. Both moneyboxes will be our secret.' She paused and smiled. 'Just as long as you tell me why Oona was staying here when I was away.'

'Do I have to?'

'Of course not. It's your choice, Joe. This is a bit like the quiz show on the TV. *Pick-a-box.* Except you get to pick between the moneyboxes and more trouble. Possibly even death.'

Joe sighed. 'Aunty Oona stayed with us because she had been hurt.'

'How was she hurt? Did she have an accident?'

Joe returned both moneyboxes to the wardrobe and closed the door. There would be no escaping Ruby's questions. 'Oona's face and her body. She had marks on her. Bruises and scratches,' he said.

'How did she get them?'

'She didn't say.'

'She must have spoken with Mum about what happened to her.'

Joe shrugged his shoulders. 'Not in front of me. I was with Char most days. They could have spoken then.'

Ruby rested a hand on her bedspread. 'Oona slept here the whole time she was over?'

'Yep. In your bed.'

'And she didn't talk about what had happened to her?'

'She didn't say, and I didn't ask.'

Ruby was about to ask her brother: why not? Why would he not want to know what had caused injuries to Oona's body? She looked across at Joe, sitting on his bed with his arms wrapped around his knees, his big brown eyes avoiding her gaze, and realised he would not have asked because he would have known the answer but wouldn't want to hear the words.

*

When breakfast was over the following morning, Ruby waited before making her move. Her mother was on her way out of the house with Joe, who had decided he'd go back to Charlie's instead of staying home with his sister. Ruby took a sleeveless frock out of the wardrobe, an apricot cotton material. She put the dress on, stood in front of the mirror, brushed her hair and tied it up in a ponytail with a white satin ribbon. People often commented that Oona dressed smartly, and Ruby wanted to impress her aunty.

She'd never been inside Oona's flat. On the only occasions she'd called by with her mother, they spoke with Oona on the front landing, which puzzled Ruby. Most visits between the sisters took place around Marion's kitchen table. Whenever Oona did visit the house, always alone, Ruby noticed that her aunty lingered into the evening. It seemed that Oona didn't want to leave and return to Ray Lomax.

Ruby had been in his presence only once, around six months earlier, when he and Oona attended a wake held at a city hotel following the funeral of Ruby and Joe's great-aunt, Bobbie Cluny. Aunty Bobbie was their grandfather's sister, and Oona's godmother. Ruby watched Ray throughout the afternoon, clutching a glass of beer in one hand and Oona's arm in the other. She noticed that when anyone tried to speak with

Oona, Ray pulled her closer to him and interrupted the conversation, putting an end to it. Ruby had just turned thirteen and she felt uncomfortable about the way Ray looked at her, staring across the room over the top of his beer glass and grinning. While he wore a new suit and had oiled his hair, Ruby noticed that Ray had yellowed teeth behind the cigarette permanently hanging from his bottom lip.

Bored with the adults talking and drinking around her, Ruby sat on a couch in the foyer of the hotel reading a women's magazine she'd found on a coffee table. A little while later Ray walked by. It was as if he'd been following her. He stopped and sat down, close enough that Ruby felt uncomfortable. He asked if she would like to join him in the garden for a cigarette. She'd never heard such a stupid question and wanted to tell Ray that he shouldn't be offering a child a cigarette. Instead, she became nervous, buried her face in the magazine and said nothing, silently praying for him to leave her alone.

Ruby felt uneasy when any man looked at her, which they'd been doing often, more recently. When she went to the shops for her mother, she avoided walking by the hotel on the corner, after a drunk had put his head out of the window and rudely stuck his tongue out at her. She also refused to shop at the closest butcher to home, Garrett's, because the apprentices behind the counter repeatedly teased her, asking if she liked meat. 'I mean real meat,' one of them had said with a smirk, causing laughter throughout the shop, on both sides of the counter. Ruby knew what they meant, without fully understanding, and felt sick.

When her mother asked why she refused to return to the butcher-shop, and Ruby told her what had been said to her, Marion left the house and stormed around the street corner into the shop. She told Mr Garrett and his boys that they should be ashamed of themselves and that she would not shop with them again. From that day onwards, Marion and Ruby trekked the half-mile to the Italian butcher further along the street.

Ruby paced the footpath outside Oona's flat. She hadn't thought about what she'd say or do if Ray Lomax opened the front door to her. She hesitated and walked along a path, around to the side of the block of flats, where she could see into the kitchen of the first-floor flat. She caught a glimpse of a person standing in the room. Clearly, it was Oona. Ruby walked back to the front of the building and climbed the flight of stairs to the flat. She straightened her frock and knocked at the door. When there was no answer, Ruby knocked a second time, a little louder. She waited, turned the handle and opened the door.

Broken glass covered the kitchen floor. A chair lay on its side beneath the table and soil from a smashed pot plant was scattered across the tabletop. Ruby hesitated, not sure what she should do. She called Oona's name and stepped as quietly into the flat as she would have a library. The refrigerator was open, and a bloodied handprint was smudged across the door. Ruby edged around the jagged pieces of glass and called Oona's name a second time. An open door on the side of the kitchen led into a hallway. Ruby walked down the hall and could see Oona sitting on an unmade bed in a room at the end of the hallway. She was holding a glass of water in her hand. Ruby moved slowly towards her aunty. When Oona looked up at her, Ruby gasped. Her face was covered in blood and was bruised. Dried blood stained the front of the dressing-gown she wore.

'Who are you and what are you doing here?' Oona asked, slurring her words. She hadn't recognised her own niece.

'I've come for a visit,' Ruby said.

Oona gave her niece the slightest nod of recognition. 'Oh, Ruby. Sorry. You'll have to come another time. I'm not well, love.'

Oona had lost a front tooth and had a deep cut below one ear. Ruby felt heat rising through her own body and sensed a bitter taste in her mouth. Her legs buckled from under her; she fell and hit her head on the corner of a narrow side table, groaned and slumped forward. Oona managed to lift herself from the bed and limped to where Ruby lay. She collapsed onto the floor beside her niece and rubbed her palm in the small of Ruby's back.

'Not you, bub. Not you.'

Ruby's memory of the events in Oona's flat that afternoon would remain vague. She'd recall the sounds of a telephone ringing incessantly throughout the flat, and Oona repeating over and over, 'That will be Ray.' Also, Ruby would recall a haunting image from the afternoon and question whether she had imagined it. Sitting on the floor beside Oona, she noticed that Oona's dressing-gown was open and there was a bloodied impression on the front of her nightie, of Oona's own face imprinted in the fabric, upside down.

'You have to get out of here,' Oona said. She put an arm around Ruby's shoulder and helped her to sit up. Ruby rested her body against the wall. 'Ray couldn't care less. A woman or a child. It makes no difference to him. It's too dangerous for you here.'

Despite her fear, Ruby could not think of leaving

Oona in the flat. 'Please, will you come with me?' she asked.

'I can't,' Oona said. 'I don't want people to see me this way.' She nudged Ruby. 'Please go.'

'But I can't,' Ruby said. 'Not without you.'

Ray Lomax had reduced Oona to a state of worthlessness, a deep sense that nobody would care for her, let alone stay by her side and risk being confronted by a monster. She couldn't make sense of Ruby's wilfulness.

'Why won't you leave?'

Ruby hadn't been certain herself. But once asked she knew the answer to Oona's question.

'I heard Mum speaking with Charlie in the yard. She told him that if she had to make the choice, she'd die for me and Joe. And that she'd die for you. Charlie said he'd do the same.' Ruby leaned into Oona. 'That's what they said.'

'But your mother and granddad are not here, love, to look after us.'

'I know,' Ruby said. 'I need you to come with me. It's what Mum would want me to do.'

Oona had only one choice left. She had to leave: if not for herself, for Ruby's safety. She struggled to her feet and shuffled back to the bedroom. Ruby helped Oona tie the dressing-gown around her waist, found a pair of slippers in the wardrobe and knelt in front of her. The toes on Oona's left foot had blackened and looked as if they'd been stood on. When Ruby put a slipper on her foot, Oona winced with pain.

'I'm sorry,' Ruby said.

Oona looked at her face in the mirror. 'Wait just a second.'

She opened her dresser drawer and took out a floral scarf and wrapped it around her head. She adjusted the scarf until her face was almost hidden.

Oona put her arms around Ruby's waist. 'If Ray sees us in the street, he'll come at me. If you see him, you take off and get home. I'm not leaving here until you promise me that. Can you do that?'

'I promise,' Ruby answered, with little conviction.

They left the flat. Oona grimaced with each step she took. The woman from the flat directly above hers was walking down the stairs as they were heading out. The woman stopped on the landing, saw the bloodstains on the front of Oona's dressing-gown, turned around and headed back upstairs.

'Old bag,' Oona muttered.

Walking slowly through the public gardens, Ruby and Oona passed people on the pathway. It was broad daylight, and no-one could have missed the terrible sight of Oona. And yet, not a single person looked either Oona or Ruby in the eye. Oona had become an invisible woman, not surprising in a neighbourhood where blindness was a skill. Oona lowered her head to save herself and those she passed further embarrassment.

They left the park and struggled along several more streets until they reached a laneway opposite the church. Oona was exhausted. 'I can't go any further,' she said. 'Leave me be. I need to sit for a while and get myself together.'

'Not here,' Ruby said. 'You can't stay here in the lane like you're rubbish.'

'But I can't go on. I've had it.'

Ruby tugged at the arm of Oona's dressing-gown. 'We can make it home from here.'

'I don't want to,' Oona admitted. 'I fought with your mother, and she told me not to come by the house if Ray was at me again. Look at the state of me. I can't let your brother see me this way. You got me out of the flat and I'm grateful. I want you to leave me be and go home.'

Ruby heard footsteps on the footpath. She turned and saw Mrs Westgarth from the church. Oona's battered face shocked the church housekeeper. She knelt beside her. 'Oh my God, you've had an accident,' she said, although it was obvious to her that Oona had been in no accident.

'You poor woman,' Mrs Westgarth added, stroking Oona's hand. 'You need to be taken to a doctor.'

'Mrs Westgarth,' Ruby said, 'if I can get Oona home the doctor will come. Can you help us?'

'Of course I will help you,' Mrs Westgarth said. 'Wait for me here. I need to go back inside and borrow the church car. I will tell Father Edmund that I need to pick up flowers for the altar. A lie,' she added, 'but not such a big one.'

She returned soon after, driving a powder-blue Morris Minor. Between herself and Ruby they managed to get Oona into the passenger seat. Ruby jumped in the back seat behind Mrs Westgarth and provided directions. They pulled up outside the house only a few minutes later.

Before helping her out of the car Mrs Westgarth spoke quietly to Oona. 'I've been looking after the church for over thirty years now, and I've seen thousands of children go through the school. I remember most of them. If not by name, all their faces.' She gently lifted a ribbon of hair from Oona's face. 'I've never forgotten you,' she said.

'Really?' Oona said.

'Yes. I can remember you marching through the gates on your first day of school, so strong, so proud of yourself. Your shining black hair bouncing from your shoulders. And I watched you over the years and you never lost that courage you have. You still have it, love. And I want to say that I'm so sorry for what has happened to you. I am truly sorry.'

'You've done nothing wrong,' Oona said. 'You haven't hurt me.'

'Maybe you're right, although I'm not certain I haven't hurt you. But I do know this. You deserve an apology from someone, and all I can do is be certain that you get it.'

'Thank you,' Oona whispered. She struggled out of the car and rested against the front gate.

Ruby thanked Mrs Westgarth for her help. 'We wouldn't have made it without you.'

'I don't know about that. You're a fierce one, Ruby. Like your mother and your aunty. You'd have found a way, I expect.'

FOURTEEN

OONA SAT ON THE FRONT step of the house and waited for Ruby to jump the side fence, climb through a window and open the door. She helped Oona inside and led her to her bedroom, where she removed her dressing-gown and laid her aunty on the bed. There were still more cuts and bruises on Oona's body.

Oona asked for a glass of water. 'My throat is burning.'

Ruby sat on the side of the bed, holding the back of Oona's head in one hand and helping her sip from the glass of water with the other. Water ran from Oona's mouth, down her chin and onto her neck. Oona asked for a Bex powder for her headache, but once she'd taken it, she gagged and vomited the powder onto the front of her nightie.

Ruby went into the kitchen and boiled the kettle. She poured the hot water into a dish and added a capful of disinfectant from a bottle she'd found in the medicine cupboard in the bathroom. She returned with the steaming bowl and a towel draped over one shoulder and a clean flannel on the other.

'You look like a nurse,' Oona said. 'My own Florence Nightingale.'

Ruby rested the dish on the dresser. The bloodstains on Oona's nightie were plastered to the wounds beneath them. Ruby wouldn't be able to treat Oona's wounds until the nightie was removed.

'We will have to take this off,' Ruby said, 'to clean the blood away from the cuts.'

Ruby gathered the hem of the nightie and gently rolled the fabric up. Oona did the best she could to raise her arms above her head and Ruby lifted the nightie, closing her eyes as she did so. The only grown woman she had seen naked was her own mother, which had not bothered either of them until Ruby reached puberty and became sensitive about her own changes. She avoided being in the bathroom at the same time as her mother. Marion understood the shift in their relationship, as she'd gone through a similar experience with her own mother when she was around Ruby's age.

Ruby opened her eyes and forced herself to look at

Oona's naked body. She was shocked to see multiple bruises in the shape of a belt buckle and a scabbing cut on one side of Oona's rib cage. The largest bruise covered Oona's left hip, in the shape of a heel. It was a horrific sight.

Ruby spoke softly to Oona, asking that she lay her head on the pillow and rest. 'Please tell me if I hurt you and I'll stop.'

Ruby began washing gently. She felt sadness for her aunty, and she was angry. She had seen the damaged bodies of children at school, and the bruised faces of women in the street, but remained unable to imagine how one person could hurt another so badly.

She began with Oona's face, methodically removing dried blood from above her mouth. She cleaned Oona's ears and wiped away the blood that had wept onto her shoulder. Ruby then sponged Oona's upper body, avoiding the cut on Oona's rib cage as it looked too tender to touch. She rinsed the flannel in the dish and washed Oona's arms and legs. The belt-buckle bruising was heaviest on Oona's thighs. Each bruise had a small cut in one corner, the result of a sharpened edge of the buckle breaking the skin. Ruby asked Oona to raise each leg just enough so she could wash her heels and the back of her calves. She bathed Oona's feet, without touching the discoloured toes on her left foot.

Oona's hands were smeared in the dried blood she'd wiped from her nose and mouth. She also had blood under her fingernails. Ruby was determined to remove every drop of blood that was the result of Ray Lomax's violence. She excused herself, went into the kitchen, searched through the pantry cupboard and found a box of toothpicks. When she returned to the room, she scraped the blood from beneath the fingernails of both of Oona's hands with a toothpick.

The colour of the water in the dish had gradually deepened from pink to red.

'I need fresh water,' Ruby explained.

She went into the kitchen and emptied the dish into the sink. It was only then that she cried. Briefly. She wiped the tears from her face with the same bloodied flannel she'd used to clean Oona's body. She filled the dish with clean water and returned to the room. Oona had fallen asleep. Her deep breaths created a soft whistling sound between her swollen lips. Ruby sat at the side of the bed. She noticed more blood in Oona's tangled hair. She parted Oona's fringe and noticed a curved-shaped cut in the centre of her forehead. When Ruby sponged the wound with the flannel, Oona opened her eyes.

'I'm cleaning your hair,' Ruby explained. 'Some of it is stuck together.' Oona moaned. 'I'm so sorry,' Ruby said. 'I'll stop.'

'Please don't,' Oona croaked. 'Touch me, please. I love it.' She rested her head on Ruby's shoulder.

Ruby took a handful of Oona's hair and sponged it with the flannel until it was free of blood. She repeated the process until Oona's hair was as clean as Ruby could manage. She put the bowl aside. She no longer feared looking at Oona's naked body. She glanced down at her own left hand. A trace of blood had caught under her fingernail.

Oona looked up at her niece. 'Make me a promise, can you, love?'

'Yes,' Ruby said. 'Anything you want.'

'Stay with me, please.'

'But you need a doctor,' Ruby said.

'I know I do. But not yet. Let me rest, please, and stay here with me.'

'I will,' Ruby said. 'Let me get something clean for you to wear.' She left the room and returned with a fresh nightie. 'This is Mum's.'

Oona sat forward and Ruby slipped the nightie over her shoulders. Oona leaned back and was soon asleep again. Ruby was also tired. She lay on Joe's bed and drifted off.

She woke several hours later, got out of bed, walked into the kitchen and checked the time on the clock above the stove. Her mother would be home in less than an hour. She picked up a kitchen chair, took it into the bedroom and sat the chair by the bed. She went to the bookshelf and picked up one of her favourite novels. *Little Women*. Sitting down on the chair she whispered to Oona, 'I'm going to read you a beautiful story.'

In a soft voice Ruby read from the novel, imagining Oona's eyes following the same words on the page. She'd always loved Friday afternoon reading time at school, when each pupil in the classroom held copies of the same book and followed the words on the page while the nun seated on the platform read aloud to them. It was the only time in the school week that the classroom was at peace. Ruby would search the faces in the room, looking for reactions from children as they read from the same passage. She would then wonder if other students were enjoying the story as much as she was.

Ruby heard the front door open. The sound woke Oona. Marion was home from work. Ruby heard her mother's footsteps and sensed her presence behind her in the doorway. Afraid to turn her head, Ruby studied Oona's face for her reaction.

Oona lifted her head from the pillow and seeing her older sister, her eyes widened. The tears that followed were not for herself, but for her sister. Oona wanted to tell Marion that she was sorry but could manage no words at all.

When Ruby turned around, her mother was gone.

Marion's rage in the kitchen was indiscriminate. She smashed the glasses and plates stacked on the drying rack on the sink. She hurled chairs and cups across the room, her favourite china teapot, knives and forks from the top drawer of the sideboard, two wooden spoons, the toaster and a pair of salt and pepper shakers that had been a wedding gift. For many years they'd been sitting innocently on top of the tallboy where Marion stored tea towels, oven gloves and hot-water bottles. She tried opening the door of the tallboy. It wouldn't comply. Marion wrestled with the cupboard, put all her strength behind it and pushed it to the floor.

'Help me up,' Oona asked Ruby. 'Your mother is destroying the house.'

'I'll go,' Ruby said, although she didn't want to go at all, fearing what she would find in the kitchen.

'Help me out of this bed,' Oona insisted. 'Now.'

Ruby assisted Oona into the kitchen. Marion's rage had passed as urgently as it had begun. She was leaning against the stove and had one hand buried in an old tea canister she hadn't used in years, which she kept out of reach on a shelf above the stove. She pulled out a packet of cigarettes and a box of matches, stuck a cigarette in her mouth and lit it.

'You don't smoke,' Ruby said, shocked at what she was seeing.

'Yes, I do,' Marion said. She drew on the cigarette and pointed it towards Oona. 'When I see my sister with her face beaten to a pulp, that's when I smoke.'

Ruby wondered if her mother had gone mad.

'Can I have a cigarette?' Oona asked.

'Sure.' Marion lit a second cigarette in her mouth, walked across the kitchen and handed it to her sister.

Oona stuck the filter in the gap left by her missing tooth and puffed gingerly. 'My mouth's so sore,' she said. She took a long drag and held the smoke in her lungs for as long as was possible. 'Jesus Christ, I love a smoke sometimes. I started on the cigarettes when I was your age,' Oona said to Ruby.

'I wouldn't allow Ruby to smoke. Not ever,' Marion said, shaking her head furiously, as if it was the only issue they need concern themselves over.

'Absolutely not,' Oona agreed. 'Don't you dare start smoking, Ruby. We'll be disappointed.'

You're both mad, Ruby thought.

Marion noticed a deep graze and swelling on the side of Ruby's face. 'Did he hit you too?' she asked.

'No, Mum. I hurt myself.'

They heard footsteps in the hallway, and Marion remembered she'd neglected to close the front door behind her. Oona flinched, for a moment convinced that Ray Lomax had arrived at the house. But it was Joe, home from Charlie's. He looked from Oona to the carnage of the room, then to his mother standing against the stove, attempting to blow a smoke ring.

Marion surprised even herself with her outward sense of composure. 'Joe,' she said, before he could say a word, 'I need you to go back to your grandfather's house and to stay there until I come for you.' She picked up her purse from the table and opened it. 'I'll give you money so you can get takeaway for tea.'

Joe looked down at the broken cups and glasses. 'What happened, Mum?'

'Nothing. An accident. Take what you need for the three of you.'

'Three of us?' he asked.

'One. Two. Three. Your grandfather, yourself and Ruby.'

'I'm not leaving,' Ruby said. 'I'm staying here with you and Oona.'

'You can't stay here,' Marion said. 'Oona needs taking care of.'

'I've taken care of Oona,' Ruby protested. 'I'm not

leaving her. Joe can go to Charlie's on his own.'

Whether Ruby would come with him or not was of no concern to Joe. He was desperate to leave the kitchen and the house and never return. He didn't want to be in a room with a broken teapot, broken chairs, with Oona's broken face and Ruby's broken heart. He wanted to be with his grandfather, in his kitchen, with his books and photographs, with the quietness of his house. He wanted to be in the backyard searching through Char's life of collecting. He turned away from his mother, his aunty and his sister, unable to look at them.

Marion opened the purse. 'Come here, Joe. You need to take this.' She handed him a ten-shilling note. 'Get the teas out of this. You can give me the change later. I'll speak with your sister, and she'll follow you soon.'

'I won't be coming,' Ruby told her brother.

'Go now, Joe,' Marion said. 'And don't you say a word to your grandfather about the mess. Not any of it.'

Joe went into his bedroom, opened the wardrobe and collected the moneybox boy. 'You're coming with me and we're never coming back here,' he explained. They left the house together.

'I need to sit down,' Oona said, gripping the back of a kitchen chair. Her face had turned deathly pale. Smoking the cigarette, stealing precious oxygen, wouldn't have helped her.

Marion again pleaded with Ruby to join Joe.

Ruby helped Oona into the chair. 'I want to stay here, Mum.'

'You're as wilful as your aunty,' Marion said. 'And look where it's got her.' Before Oona could protest, Marion apologised. 'I'm sorry. It was stupid of me to say that. It's not what I meant.'

Marion lit another cigarette and sat at the table. Her family was in danger of falling apart, and she wouldn't allow that to happen. By the time she'd finished smoking her second cigarette, she'd decided what she would need to do if Oona was to have any chance of surviving Ray Lomax. She butted the stub of the cigarette in the bottom of a broken teacup.

'Ruby, sit with your aunty in the front room,' Marion said. 'And I'll clean this mess away.'

'Let me help you,' Ruby offered.

'No, I won't have it. I'm responsible for this, and I need to fix it. Keep your aunty company and watch some TV. And Oona, as soon as I've done what's needed, I'm getting a doctor in.'

Oona opened her mouth to speak but was stopped

by her sister's forcefulness. 'Don't argue with me. Either of you.'

After thoroughly cleaning the kitchen Marion went into the front room. 'You listen to me carefully,' she said to Ruby. 'If you won't go and chase after your brother, at least help me out here. Do you understand me?'

Ruby nodded her head in agreement.

'I need you to stay here with your aunty while I'm out of the house. You need to turn the TV off now. And no radio and no lights. You can't make a sound. We need the house dead quiet. Is that clear?'

'Where are you going?' Ruby asked.

'Ruby, I asked you if what I said to you is clear and nothing more. Do you understand me?'

'Yes, Mum.'

'The front and back doors, keep them locked. Do you understand that also?' Marion said.

'I do.'

'Can you answer her question, please?' Oona said. 'Where are you going, Marion? And why do we have to be so quiet?'

Marion couldn't believe her sister would ask such a question. She'd have preferred that she not be forced to explain herself in front of Ruby but had little choice but to do so.

'Because he'll come looking for you, sooner or later. Ray Lomax.'

'Why?'

'You've seen your face in the mirror? The damage?'

'Of course I have.'

'Right. The last time you were here, you hid the damage as best you could. And you did a decent job of it. But this.' She pointed to her sister's face. 'It can't be hidden from anyone, whatever disguise you wear. Ray Lomax can't be shown up on the street for what he is. He'll want you kept away, in the flat, until all this is gone.'

'But people know.' Oona sighed. 'They always know.'

'Sure do, love. But he won't want them seeing. And that's all that matters. So, please, both of you, sit quiet until I get back.'

FIFTEEN

THE ENTRANCE TO THE CRIMSON Club was by way of a side door and a climb up two flights of narrow stairs to the second floor, above a furniture retailer. The front room was decorated with deep-red wallpaper, dark wood and low-lit chandeliers. A house band played four nights a week, and the bar served only spirits, watered down, at double the price of any hotel. The big money was made in a windowless second room, where a baccarat game operated six nights a week from ten at night until five the next morning.

Stan Curtis had been running the club for eight years. He oversaw the card game, watchful of every transaction. An outwardly unemotional man, he never lost his temper, rare in a trade where a hair-trigger was common. Stan had only two interests in life: the club and making money.

He'd met Marion Cluny fifteen years earlier, when he was pencilling for an SP bookmaker and she was only weeks into her first job, behind the counter of the dry-cleaning shop. Stan had always worn a suit, even when he was younger, when most men were happy to get about in overalls and a singlet. He came into the cleaners each week to have one of his suits pressed. Marion didn't think that Stan had anything particular to offer except that he was clean and spoke politely enough.

They'd been going out together for only a few months when she became pregnant. Marion thought about an abortion and knew of several women in the suburb who offered their services. Having been raised a Catholic didn't put her off. Several girls she'd been at school with had had at least one. It was fear that stopped Marion. Hardly a year passed without stories circulating about women who'd suffered terribly after an infection following an abortion, including women who'd died.

Stan offered to marry her, and without too much thought Marion said yes, to her parents' relief. Charlie and Ada would have hoped for someone better for their daughter. But they preferred Stan to the alternative of Marion being left as an unwed single mother, which would have left them feeling shameful. When Ruby was born, named after his late mother, Stan doted over the baby, parading her in a pram along the main street, dressed in expensive outfits from a city boutique. By the time Joe came along, the novelty of having his own children had worn off and Stan decided he wasn't suited to family life. It interfered with his career, a steady rise in the gambling world, a nocturnal profession. Little more than a year after Joe's birth, Stan left and only saw his growing children occasionally.

Marion stood at the bottom of the stairs, gathered her thoughts and walked up the two flights of creaking stairs. The iron door at the top of the second floor was open, and Stan's offsider, Billy Keen, was sitting inside on a velvet couch enjoying a cigar. When he saw Marion, he jumped up and kissed her on both cheeks.

'Look who it is. Wonderful to see you, Marion. You're too good for this haunt. You know for a minute I mistook you for Grace Kelly. Then I looked again and remembered that she's not up to your class.'

Marion gestured at her work uniform. 'Don't go overboard with the charm, Billy. I haven't come to see you.'

'That's no good. The dancing will start a little later.'

Billy would have worn a welcoming face, were it not for the scar on one cheek, running from his left eye to the corner of his lip. Over the years he'd told many tales about the origins of the scar, none of which were true.

'You'd remember how good a dancer I am,' Billy said, swaying his more than ample hips from side to side.

While Marion had never minded Billy's boyish humour, she didn't have the patience for it. 'I need to see Stan. It's urgent, Billy.'

'I don't know if we can do that,' Billy said. 'He's in a meeting with Arnold. They only just got going and it usually takes them an hour or so to wind up. When Stan's with his accountant, he doesn't like to be disturbed. These meetings are as sacred as confession.'

'It's about Ruby,' Marion said. 'Let him know she's in trouble.'

Billy appeared genuinely alarmed. 'Your Ruby is a beauty. I'll step up now if you need me to.'

'Thanks for the offer, Billy. But no. This needs to be on Stan. Her father. Please go and tell him we need to talk.'

Billy was in and out of Stan's office within minutes. 'Come on through. He'll see you now.'

Stan was standing behind a narrow desk in an office little bigger than a bathroom. Cardboard boxes, reaching close to the ceiling, were stacked against the walls of the room. Stan's street-educated accountant, Arnold Roy, was seated on an upturned fruit box. His fingers danced across the keys of a calculating machine. Arnold was a touch over five feet tall and was so thin he couldn't have found work as a paperweight.

'What's wrong with Ruby?' Stan asked, clearly agitated.

Marion looked across at Arnold. 'We need to talk in private, Stan.'

Stan dismissed the accountant with the wave of a hand and waited until he'd closed the door before sitting down and asking, 'She's not pregnant, is she?'

The comment startled Marion. 'Ruby is only thirteen years old, Stan. Of course she's not pregnant.'

'I'm sorry,' he said. 'I thought she might be fifteen or sixteen.'

'You don't even know how old your own daughter is? And would it make it okay if she was fifteen?'

'No. It wouldn't,' Stan said. 'Calm down. I said I was sorry. Tell me what's up with her?'

'Ruby's fine. I lied to Billy so I could get in here to see you. I need to talk to you about Oona.'

Stan frowned. 'You've come up here to talk to me about your sister? Oona's old enough to take care of herself.'

'Can I sit down,' Marion asked. 'I've had it.'

Looking at his wristwatch, Stan said, 'I don't have a lot of time. Arnie likes to get home to his wife in time for his dinner. He's late as it is.'

Marion sat on the fruit box and slipped off her heels. 'Oona's at my place with Ruby.' She leaned forward. She hadn't been so physically close to Stan for years. 'Do you know a fella by the name of Ray Lomax?'

Stan straightened his back and grimaced slightly, just enough for Marion to know that she'd hit a nerve of some kind.

'I don't know him personally,' Stan said. 'He's got the electrical business on the strip. Picked it up from his father when the old man died. I don't know a lot more about him than that.'

Marion smiled at her ex-husband. Stan had to be lying. He didn't know a little about anyone. Stan made it his business to know everything about anyone who crossed his path and stored the information in his rat-trap memory for future use.

'That's him,' Marion said. 'Did you know that he and Oona live together?'

'Really? I've seen the two of them in here a couple of times but didn't know it was serious. But I don't pay too much attention to the lovebirds that come in. I run a nightclub, not a dating agency. I wouldn't have thought he'd be Oona's type. Your sister.' He raised his eyebrows. 'Well, there you go.'

'What do you mean by that, Stan?'

'Well, she likes to get out and about. Dress up. Look the part.'

'Look what part, Stan?'

Stan raised his hands in the air. 'Take it easy. I don't have the time for this. What do you want from me?'

'I don't have time to waste either,' Marion said. 'A couple of days ago Ray Lomax beat my sister close to death. That's why she's at my place now, hiding from him with cuts and bruises all over her body. I can't have her going back to him. He's done this to her before, more than once, and if he's not stopped, he'll do it again. The man could kill her.'

Stan shifted awkwardly in his chair. 'I'm sorry to hear that. It doesn't surprise me. Ray has a look about him.'

'What do you mean?'

'The way he carries himself.'

'The men who beat women up have a look, do they, Stan? I wish you'd mentioned this to me years ago. Do you think you could give me a description of the type of man to look out for? I'll issue a public warning.' Marion leaned towards Stan. 'Something needs to be done. Ray has to be stopped.'

'Stopped by who?'

'Why do you think I'm here? You, of course. Or Billy Keen out there. Or any one of the men who work for you. I don't care who does it. I need my sister protected before she's killed.' Marion didn't want to beg for Stan's help but felt she had little choice. 'It will get desperate for Oona from here. If he hadn't worked it out already, soon enough Ray will know that she's back at my house and he'll come looking for her. We need help.'

Stan had no interest in getting involved in another man's personal business. 'I can't do anything about it,' he said. 'You should know better than to ask me. This is a domestic.'

'It's not a domestic, Stan. It's violence. And Oona is my sister. My blood. Your own children's blood.'

Stan raised a hand in the air again. 'If Ray Lomax laid a hand on one of my children, I wouldn't hesitate. You wouldn't need to come here and ask me. It would be done before you walked up these stairs. But what happens between him and Oona cannot be a concern of mine. And you should know why without me having to explain it to you.'

Marion shook her head. 'I can't believe this. I'm talking about my own sister, Stan. Does this mean nothing to you? She's family.'

'She's not my family,' Stan said. 'And hasn't been for years.'

'What about your own children?' Marion said. 'They live in the same house. How do I protect them when Ray's after Oona and turns up on my doorstep?'

Stan smiled. 'That weasel would know better than to touch my kids,' he said. 'If you're so worried about Ruby and Joe, all you need to do is tell your sister to get back home where she belongs and sort out her problems with Ray.'

'That's all you have to say to me?' Marion asked. 'That she goes back to the man who smashed her face in? Thank you, Stan. You care about nobody but yourself. I want you to know that if anything more happens to Oona, I'll make sure Ruby and Joe know that I came to you for help, and you turned me away.'

Stan didn't doubt Marion would be true to her word. He didn't want his kids feeling more poorly of him than they already did. He was known around the streets for making deals. He would have to give Marion something she could walk away with, with her pride intact.

'Okay,' he said. 'Enough please. I'll do what I can to help you out. I'll get Billy to have a serious word with Ray. Let him know that he's not to come by your place unless he wants trouble with me. If Ray needs to sort himself out with your sister, he'll have to arrange to meet her elsewhere.' He again looked at his watch. 'We'll have to leave it there.'

'That's it?' Marion said. 'You're going to get your messenger boy to have a word in Ray Lomax's ear? That will go a long way. Oona will never be able to walk the street without the fear of being murdered by him.'

Marion found herself distracted momentarily by the cardboard boxes stacked behind Stan's desk. She noticed the brand name and the illustration on the boxes, and realised they contained the same portable radios she'd seen in the window of Ray Lomax's electrical goods shop.

'You bastard, Stan,' she said.

'Knock it off,' he said. 'Don't be talking to me that way because I choose to mind my own business.'

'I get it now. You're not prepared to raise a hand over Ray Lomax's treatment of my sister because you're in business with him. He's moving these record players for you, and you don't want to harm your interest. You're gold, Stan.'

Stan glanced over his shoulder at the boxes. 'For a good Catholic girl, it's only ever taken you a short time to spot the graft, Marion. I don't know if you should have been police or a career crim.'

He stood up, took hold of Marion's arm and guided her towards the doorway.

'It's time for you to leave, Marion. Whatever business interests I have with Ray Lomax has nothing to do with my decision. Your sister should have known better than to get around with him in the first place. Ray had form when it comes to knocking women around. Everybody knew it. Except for your sister, yourself and your slow-witted father. Ray might be a problem for you. But he's not mine.'

'Let go of my arm, Stan.' Marion shook herself free of him. 'And get fucked.'

Billy smiled at her on her way out of the club. 'We'll see you another night, love,' he said.

'Don't count on it, Billy.'

Early that same evening Charlie had been working in the front yard, turning over a garden bed. Joe ran towards him, dropped the moneybox on the ground and threw himself at his grandfather.

'Hey, you're back. What's wrong with you?' Charlie asked.

'Aunty Oona. She's been hurt again.'

Charlie's heart sank. He took Joe by the hand and sat with him on the front step of the verandah. Joe ran the palms of his hands down his face, wiping tears away. He hadn't washed up after working with Charlie earlier, and both cheeks were quickly covered in grime.

'Look at you,' Charlie said. 'You look like your friend over there lying in the garden bed. Come inside and I'll clean you up.'

'Wait,' Joe said. He ran and retrieved the moneybox. He wiped a spot of dirt from the boy's face and carried him in his arms.

In the bathroom, Joe put his hands under the tap and Charlie passed him a bar of soap, all the while thinking about what he was going to do once he'd settled his grandson. Once Joe was clean, Charlie passed him a towel. They went back into the kitchen and Charlie sat him in the reading chair. 'How about a treat?' he asked. 'A hot chocolate made with warm milk?'

'Yes please,' Joe said, nursing the moneybox. He watched his grandfather fill two cups with chocolate powder and heat the milk.

Charlie turned around and looked at the moneybox. 'I see you've brought the young fella you painted your face in honour of. How'd he find his way to your place?'

'I felt sorry for him being alone at school, so I put him in my bag on the last day of school and brought him home. He's been living in the wardrobe,' Joe added, as if the theft made perfect sense.

'Did he have coins inside him when you brought him home?'

'No,' Joe explained. 'I emptied his stomach and put the money on Sister's desk.'

'Good,' Charlie said. 'I like that.' He passed Joe a cup of hot chocolate. 'Now. Tell me what's happened to Oona.'

'I don't know much,' Joe said. 'She looks really hurt and Mum smashed our kitchen.'

'She smashed her own kitchen up?'

'She was angry. And afraid too. Oona's boyfriend might kill her, Char.'

'That won't be happening,' Charlie said, remaining calm for his grandson's sake. 'I need to fix this. Don't you worry. Oona will be safe, and your mother.' He wrapped both hands around his cup. 'Where's Ruby now?'

'She's at the house with them. Mum told her to come here with me, but she wouldn't budge.'

'I'm not surprised,' Charlie said. 'The Cluny women. They're all the same.'

Charlie left Joe in the reading chair sipping his warm drink and went into the yard. He'd stored the revolver wrapped in the oiled cloth in one of his toolboxes. He unwrapped the cloth and held the gun in his hand for some time, mulling over what he would do. He made his decision and went back into the house.

'I have to go out for a few minutes,' he explained. 'I had so many jobs on today that I forgot to finish one. You'll need to stay here.'

Joe didn't want his grandfather to leave him alone in the house. 'Can you do the work tomorrow, Char?'

'I wish I could, Joe, but I promised this fella I'd get this final job finished for him.' For perhaps the first time in their relationship Joe could read his grandfather's mind. He knew that there was more to what Char was up to, something secretive, but couldn't work out what it was.

'I expect you must be hungry,' Charlie said. 'There's half a loaf in the bread drawer and cheese and butter in the refrigerator. Make yourself a sandwich.'

Joe felt too anxious to eat. 'No, thank you, Char.'

'Please yourself. If I'm not back before bedtime,' Charlie said, 'you go in the front room, get in your nanna's bed and read a book.' He hugged his grandson. 'I love you.'

'I love you too, Char.'

After Charlie left the house Joe searched through the bookcase. The novels had now been fully sorted into alphabetical order and occupied three shelves. On the bottom shelf were cookery books, atlases and a book containing colour plates of migratory birds from across the world. He picked the bird book up, went back to the reading chair and opened it.

Each bird listed in the book was accompanied by a colour plate of a male and female of the species. A map, marked with red dotted lines, tracked their flight paths and journeys from the northern hemisphere to the south and back again the following year. Some birds made their nests in trees, some in scrub and others in grasslands on the edge of the ocean. Joe put a fingertip on a point where one of the species began its flight below the Arctic Circle. He traced the journey of the bird with his finger, across land and water, over thousands of miles until it arrived at the place where it would meet up with its mate, in the Southern Ocean. Joe could see his own city on the map, near the place where the birds nested each year. The pair remained together and only left when their young had grown strong enough to fly and care for themselves. Joe read the last line of one entry several times. *The survival of the tern is dependent on courage and intelligence.* He placed the book in his lap and tried to imagine what would drive a small creature to fly so far.

*

Charlie drove to the scrapyard and arrived as Ranji was closing the iron gates to go home for the night. Charlie wound down his side window. 'I'm sorry for coming by so late,' he said, 'but I need something from you.'

'I work late in the summer,' Ranji said. 'This is no problem for me. Drive into the yard.' Ranji could see that his friend was agitated. Charlie got out of the car, unwrapped the revolver from the cloth and pointed it towards Ranji, who raised his hands above his head and smiled. 'If you're going to shoot me, Charlie, you will need the bullets.'

'I do need the bullets,' he said. 'That's why I've come.'

'I don't believe I need to give you the bullets for this gun. Why would you require them, Charlie?'

'Because I need to shoot someone.'

'Is this a joke of yours?' Ranji asked. 'You drove all the way here to play a practical joke on me?'

'I'm not joking,' Charlie shouted in anger.

Ranji realised that his friend was serious. 'You are too good a person to shoot anyone,' he said. 'What is happening to you?'

'Don't patronise me,' Charlie said. 'Not you, Ranji. Give me the fucking bullets to this gun. Now. Before I change my mind.'

Ranji raised his open hands and walked towards

him. 'Charlie. Charlie. What has happened to you? Please come inside and sit. We can talk.'

Charlie refused to move. Ranji wrapped an arm around his friend and guided him into his office. 'Come on,' he said, quietly. 'Let's sit and you can explain to me why you need these bullets and who it is that you are going to shoot. If you show me a good reason, I will give you the bullets. My promise.'

Charlie had not spoken to Ranji about Oona's previous stay at Marion's house or told him that she'd been beaten by Ray Lomax. He sat in a rickety chair in Ranji's office, went over the story and told him about Joe running to his house that evening.

'This will never stop,' Charlie said. 'I've seen this in other men. They don't stop until they've killed someone in their own family. Until something is done to stop him, Oona's life is in danger. I can't let that happen to my daughter.' He held out an open hand. 'Please, Ranji, give me the bullets.'

'I wish you had told me about this earlier,' Ranji said.

'And what would that have done?' Charlie said.

'I'm not certain that I could have done anything,' Ranji said. 'At least you would have had a friend to confide in. The silence that you have been living with can only hurt you.'

'I know,' Charlie said. 'It's hurt all of us. For too long. It's too late for that now.' He rapped his knuckles on the desk. 'The bullets. Please.'

Ranji shook his head. 'You are too gentle a man to kill another person, Charlie. And, even if you were able to do so, would you like to spend the rest of your life in prison, locked away from your family? From that beautiful boy? Joe loves you and he will need you to be around as he grows to be a man himself. He needs the gentleness in you, not the violence that this man has caused your family.'

In his anger, Charlie had given no consideration to the impact that attempting to kill Ray Lomax would have on his family. Nor had he considered the stark reality addressed by Ranji: that he was incapable of killing anyone, even to save his daughter's life. The revelation was immediate, and it deflated him.

He slumped in the chair. 'Fuck. I'm not capable of protecting my own daughter.'

'This man is a threat to your Oona, I agree.' Ranji thought about what could be done. 'I know what we will do,' he said. 'Oona will come to my home and stay with my wife and myself. Away from the trouble.'

'Your house? The trouble we have with this man is not yours, Ranji. I can't involve you in this shit.'

'This man who is a danger to you is my concern. To

be honest with you, Charlie, having now heard what he has done to your daughter, had you screamed at me one more time to give you the bullets, I would most likely have given them to you. I would have driven you myself, to shoot this man.'

'But you just told me I was no killer.'

'That is correct,' Ranji said. 'But possibly, I am.'

'I don't think so,' Charlie said.

'You may be right. But who knows?' He raised his eyebrows. 'Whatever. I think that having your daughter at my home is a better outcome for all.'

'You would need to speak to your wife about Oona,' Charlie said. 'This could be a problem for her?'

'It will be no problem at all. My two sons have moved away, and we have spare rooms. My wife would love to have another woman in the house. It will mean that she doesn't have to talk so much with me.'

'You live miles away from here,' Charlie said.

'Yes, I do. Which will work in our favour. My home will be a safe place for your daughter. This Ray will not know where to search for her.'

With no other option available to his family, Ranji's offer was the best that Charlie had. 'Are you sure about this?'

'I am certain. I will speak with my wife when I arrive home tonight. And you will bring Oona here tomorrow morning and we will drive her to my home together. Yes?'

'Yes,' Charlie said. 'Thank you, Ranji.'

'I want you to leave the gun with me,' Ranji said.

'But there's no need to, without bullets.'

'That's true. Technically. But I will rest more comfortably knowing that you are not waving this gun around in that man's face. He would most likely take it from you and hit you over the head with it.'

The men embraced, and Charlie left the scrapyard and drove home.

Joe had fallen asleep in the reading chair. Charlie collected the book from his grandson's lap and returned it to the bookcase. He went into the room and turned back the blankets on his and Ada's bed. Back in the kitchen he lifted Joe into his arms, carried him into the bedroom and laid him down, covering him with the blankets. Charlie realised how tired he was. He hesitated for a moment before lying on top of the covers alongside Joe. He turned towards his grandson and was soon asleep.

SIXTEEN

MARION WALKED HOME THROUGH THE darkened streets with little idea of what she would do next. She hadn't expected too much help from her ex-husband but left the Crimson Club with nothing at all. It would be only a matter of time before Ray came to the house searching for Oona. There was now nothing that Marion could do to stop him.

'Where did you get to?' Oona asked, when Marion arrived home.

Marion was exhausted. She sat in a lounge chair and rested her face in her hands. 'It doesn't matter. I wasted my time going out. Where's Ruby?'

'She fell asleep on your bed. I wanted to sit up and wait for you.'

'I'll have to get her up. We can't stay here tonight.

It will be best if we leave.'

'And go where?' Oona asked.

'We can spend the night at Dad's and tomorrow we'll work something out. Get you away from here.'

Oona wasn't having it. 'I'm not going to Dad's and I'm not going anywhere. I need to find my own place, and it will be around here. I'm not leaving because of Ray.'

'You can't stay around here,' Marion said. 'He'll be looking for you.'

'I don't care. Fuck him. I'm not running away. I grew up here and I'm staying.'

'And how will you manage that. Have you got a plan?' Marion asked. 'Anything more than *fuck him*?'

'Right now, I'm dead tired and I want to go to bed.'

'That's it?' Marion asked.

'For now, it is. Let me have one night's peace and we can talk about this in the morning.'

'And a doctor? Will you see one?'

'Yes. I promise you,' Oona said. 'Can we share a bed tonight – you, me and Ruby?'

'Of course. That would be nice,' Marion said, although she was thinking more about Ruby's protection, not being left in a room on her own.

Marion locked the back door and followed her sister

into the front bedroom. Oona lay on one side of the bed. Marion pulled the blind down and got into the other side, with Ruby between them, asleep.

'This is cosy,' Marion said, attempting a smile. She could hear music playing further along the street, and a dog barking in the distance.

'I'm so sorry,' Oona whispered.

'There's nothing you need to be sorry for,' Marion said. 'You might not agree with me, but this must be said now, Oona. Until you understand that none of this is your fault, that you have done nothing wrong, little will change for you. Ray Lomax is a no-good dog. It's as simple as that. Now please go to sleep.'

Marion lay thinking about the mistake she'd made approaching Stan in the way she had, asking him to deal with Ray on her behalf. Stan Curtis was concerned with the business of money and little else. She should have asked him for cash. Enough for Oona to get safely away from Ray. She decided she'd return to the club the following evening and wouldn't utter a word of complaint about Stan's dealings with Ray Lomax. She'd ask for a loan to help Oona, so that she could move across to the other side of the river. Or interstate, if necessary. Marion felt confident that Stan would welcome such an arrangement. Regardless of her ability to repay the money, she was confident that Stan would provide her with a loan. Having his ex-wife in his debt would sit well with Stan Curtis.

Ray Lomax didn't bother knocking at the front door. He kicked it in. Marion woke terrified, sat up and shook Ruby and Oona awake. Ruby was quick out of the bed, but Oona struggled and fell to the floor. Ruby helped her to her feet, and the three of them escaped as far as the kitchen. Marion was fumbling to get the key in the back door. It dropped to the floor at the moment Ray stormed into the room.

'Here you are, Oona.' He smiled. 'Thank God. I've been worrying myself sick about you.'

'Get out of my house,' Marion screamed. 'You're not welcome here.'

'Welcome?' Ray laughed. 'Don't worry. I wasn't expecting a welcome from you. I've come to pick up Oona and get out of your way.' He reached for Oona's hand. She backed away, to the opposite side of the room. 'Come on,' he growled. 'I didn't come here to play cat and mouse.'

'I'm asking you to leave my house,' Marion insisted. 'If you lay a hand on my sister, I'll be straight to the police station.'

'That's a good idea,' Ray said. 'See what good it

will do you. The police earn from my business. And they won't give up a regular purse from me over an argument with Oona. If you want the police on your side, you'll need to find enough cash to put them in your pocket. I'd outbid you in small change.'

'It wasn't an argument you had, Ray. It was a beating,' Marion said. 'You belted my sister senseless.'

'She looks alright to me,' Ray smirked.

Ruby put her hands over her ears. 'Please stop,' she cried. 'Stop.'

Oona could be heard reciting the same words over and over. 'I'm sorry, Marion. Ruby. I'm sorry.'

Witnessing the pain on her sister's face and the fear in her daughter, Marion felt that all she could do was to try reasoning with Ray. Flatter him, even. She had to get Oona safely out of the house and away from him, whatever the cost.

'Can I ask something of you,' she said politely. 'Please, Ray.'

'Ask whatever you like,' he answered. 'It will make no difference. Oona is coming home with me.'

'I understand that,' Marion said. 'And I don't want to interfere.'

'Neither you fucking should.'

'Oona's not well,' Marion said. 'You can see that yourself. She needs a rest and she needs care. I can give her that. As soon as she's well, she'll come home to you, in the next few days.' Marion gazed pleadingly at her sister. 'Won't you, love?'

Oona was aware of what Marion was trying to do to protect her. She also knew it would have no impact on Ray's state of mind. She sensed his growing agitation. He was about to explode, and Oona couldn't allow either her sister or niece to be harmed by him. She looked lovingly at Marion, a guardian angel who had always done whatever was necessary to protect her. Oona then turned to Ruby, whose piercing dark eyes were fixed on Ray.

'I'm ready to come home with you, Ray,' she said. 'I just need to get a few things from the bedroom, and we can go home together and talk. We do need to talk, Ray,' she added. 'You understand that, don't you?'

Ray felt a sense of victory over the women. 'Of course. We'll have a good chat when we're back at the flat. Maybe a drink.'

'No. No,' Marion begged her sister. 'Please, Oona. You don't have to go with him.'

Ray slammed a fist on the table. 'Keep your fucking head out of this. You heard what your sister just said. She wants to come with me.'

Marion ignored him and spoke softly to her sister. 'Listen to me. Please listen, Oona. You don't have to leave with him. I can't let you do that.' She paused. 'I know why you're doing this, and I don't want you to. Not this way. Whatever is going to happen, all I know is we need to stick by each other and go through it together. Ray, please,' she said. 'My daughter, Ruby. Will you let her leave the house? I don't want her to see this.'

'Stop, Marion. Stop,' Oona pleaded. 'I understand what you're trying to do. And I love you for it. I really do. But I have to leave now. It's best for all of us.'

'Fuck the both of you!' Ray shouted. 'Oona! We're leaving now.'

Ruby suddenly screamed at Ray. 'You're not having her! I cleaned Oona's body, and you can't take her away from me now and make her dirty again. You can't hurt her again.' She charged at Ray.

Marion reached for her daughter's hand as Ray swung an arm and backhanded Ruby with a force that knocked her to the floor. He grabbed Oona by the arm. 'We're leaving!'

Marion looked down at her daughter. 'Please don't cry,' she said, realising, even as she spoke the words, that what she'd said made no sense.

Ruby looked up at her mother. She didn't cry at all. Blood ran from both nostrils into her mouth. In that moment, she experienced a most random thought, which for days after would puzzle her. Ruby could feel her heart pounding in her chest and recalled a lesson from a science class that explained that a gallon of blood would pass through her heart each minute she lay on her back.

Marion collected the key from the floor and managed to unlock the back door. 'Go. Go,' she screamed at her daughter. 'To your grandfather. Now!'

She pulled her daughter to her feet. Ruby didn't question her mother's frantic demand. She ran out of the kitchen, into the yard, and scrambled over the back fence.

Ray had dragged Oona into the hallway. Marion kept a small axe by the laundry door that she used to chop the wood for the chip heater. She picked the axe up and ran into the hallway. Ray had one hand under Oona's armpit, lifting her body from the floor. Marion swung the blunt end of the axe at him. It smashed into his shoulder. Ray screamed out in pain, released Oona and clutched at his arm. Marion swung the axe a second time. It hit Ray in the side of the head. He fell to his knees and slammed his face into the floor. The vibration appeared to shift the house.

Oona looked down at Ray. He tried lifting himself from the floor. Blood from the open wound on the side of his head wept onto the floorboards. Attempting to crawl forward, Ray slipped in his own blood. In desperation, he reached for Oona with his hand, clawing at her ankle.

Years earlier, when Marion had just moved into the house, Oona decided to make her sister a housewarming gift. A decorated doorstop that she'd made from a brick sourced from her father's backyard. She'd decorated it with floral material. The doorstop had remained in its place ever since, behind the front door, the sewn cover frayed and grubby, and now almost falling apart.

Ray groaned; a guttural sound, like a dying animal. Oona picked up the doorstop and looked at her sister. Marion nodded her head, ever so slightly. Oona felt the weight of the brick in her hand. It comforted her.

Ruby had sprinted along the side of her grandfather's house to the kitchen door. The reading chair, where she expected to find either Charlie or Joe, was empty. She went into the bedroom. The pair were asleep on the bed. Joe under the covers, her grandfather on top of them, one arm draped across Joe's body. The moneybox boy sat on a small table next to the bed, gazing in Ruby's direction. The boy appeared content with himself.

Ruby moved towards her grandfather. His face was

soft and peaceful. Ruby, unable to bear the thought of him being hurt by Ray Lomax, looked up at a photograph of her grandmother above the bed and backed out of the room. She returned to the kitchen and knelt beside the reading chair. Ruby clasped her hands together. She prayed to God to help her mother and Oona, and she asked that He punish Ray Lomax for the many sins he had committed against Oona.

When Joe woke the next morning, he was alone in his grandfather's bed. He lay on his back and stared up at the ceiling. The plaster had cracked over the years and a spider-web pattern spread across the room. He got out of the bed, nursing the moneybox boy under his arm. In the kitchen he found Ruby asleep in the reading chair under a blanket. She opened her eyes.

'What are you doing in Char's chair?' he asked.

'I came here to look after you. You were asleep with Charlie in Nanna's bed. I left you and came out here to read. I must have fallen asleep.'

'And where is Char now?'

'I don't know,' Ruby said. 'Maybe he's in the yard cleaning up.'

Joe noticed the time on the clock above the stove. 'Today is our first day at the new school,' he said. 'Are we going?'

'Not today. Our Lady's doesn't start back for another week.'

'But we're going to the new state school,' Joe said. 'And it starts today.'

'You might be,' Ruby said. 'I've changed my mind. I'm staying with the nuns.'

'Why?'

'Mrs Westgarth. I'd really miss her,' Ruby said.

Joe was puzzled. 'You'll miss the cleaning lady?'

'Yep. The cleaning lady.'

Joe put the moneybox boy on the kitchen table and perched on the arm of the reading chair next to his sister. He wanted to ask her about Oona and their mother, but couldn't bring himself to do so, fearful of the answer.

Ruby sensed her brother's concern. 'Oona will be safe now.'

'How could you know that?' Joe said.

'Because I prayed for her to be taken care of. And she will be.'

'Do you know that for sure?'

'I know nothing for sure. But I believe it.'

It was very early morning when Charlie's wagon drove slowly through the still-dark streets of the suburb he'd kept clean for decades. He'd phoned Ranji earlier and the scrapman had left his bed and driven across the city in the night to his yard. Once Charlie arrived, Ranji opened the gates and bolted them after the wagon was inside.

Charlie got out of the car. 'You don't need to be here any longer,' he said. 'You can go back home now, Ranji, and leave me to bolt the gates when I'm done.'

'I'm going nowhere,' Ranji said. 'I'm here to help you.'

'I don't need your help, and I don't want you getting yourself involved. This is my business, not yours.'

'I made this my business by driving here. Let's not waste time, Charlie.'

'Are you sure you want to do this?'

'I think it's best not to ask,' Ranji said. 'If we begin questioning ourselves, it may be that neither of us will be able to do what must be done.'

Afterwards, the two friends sat together in front of Ranji's office. Charlie looked at his wristwatch and asked, 'What time do you need to pray?'

'There will be no prayers,' Ranji answered. 'Not today.'

Marion stood in the kitchen wearing a dressing-gown. The hallway had been thoroughly cleaned and a distinct scent of bleach filled the air. Earlier, Marion had washed blood from both her own and Oona's body, gently sponging her sister's face and hands, just as Ruby had done.

After helping Oona into bed Marion had inspected her own body in the bathroom mirror, determined to remove all trace of the man who had brought intimidation into her home. She walked into her bedroom and looked down at Oona asleep. Marion pulled the bedspread back and slipped under the covers, alongside her younger sister. Oona's skin was warm. Marion wrapped herself around her sister, cradling her just as she had done when Oona was a small child. Oona stirred, feeling the comfort of Marion's breath on her skin.

'I love you,' Marion whispered. 'I love you.'

AUTHOR'S NOTE

WOMEN & CHILDREN IS A work of fiction. It is not the story of my own family, but a story motivated by our family's refusal to accept silence as an option in our lives. It is a story that witnesses both the trauma of violence and the freedom that comes with summary justice, even when satisfaction is a momentary experience. I want to thank my grandmother, my mother and my daughters for their inherent courage; my mother, Dawn, particularly, who has never taken prisoners. And I want to remind my brothers that we were once children and not damaged men. There was a time in our lives when, like Joe Cluny, we were the sweetest of boys and we deserved something more.

Women & Children is for the women in my life, and in memory of two almost-forgotten men: Bhouta

Khan, my great-grandfather (by marriage), and Les 'Ranji' Moodie, my great-uncle, a champion boxer and an even better man. The photograph on the cover of the novel is of my late aunty and godmother, Maureen, and my eldest sister, Debbie, on the day of her first communion. I thank Debbie and my cousin Kerrie (Maureen's daughter) for their permission to use the photograph. I also thank the photographer, my mother, Dawn.

The completion of this novel would not have been possible without the support of my publisher, Aviva Tuffield, who sometimes knows better than I do what it is that I am attempting to write. As does Yasmin Smith, a wonderful young editor I have been fortunate to work with for the first time. The cover of *Women & Children* was designed by the wonderful Jenna Lee, who I have worked with now on many of my books. I'm the lucky boy.

I want to thank Sara for her love and her big, big heart; Kes the Wonder-Dog for his loyalty and madness; and Erin, Siobhan, Drew, Grace and Nina for their generosity. My children are amazing. I want to offer a shout-out to my sons-in-law, Nick and Dan, who are wonderful fathers, and good and gentle fellas. I now have four grandchildren: Isabel, Archie, Charlie and Louis. I want them to one day understand that although I'm finally at peace with my childhood, I'm so happy that their own lives are less dramatic. I could tell them I love them on the hour, every hour of the day, and yet my words would fail to convey the depth of my feelings towards them. They are in my body as I am in theirs.

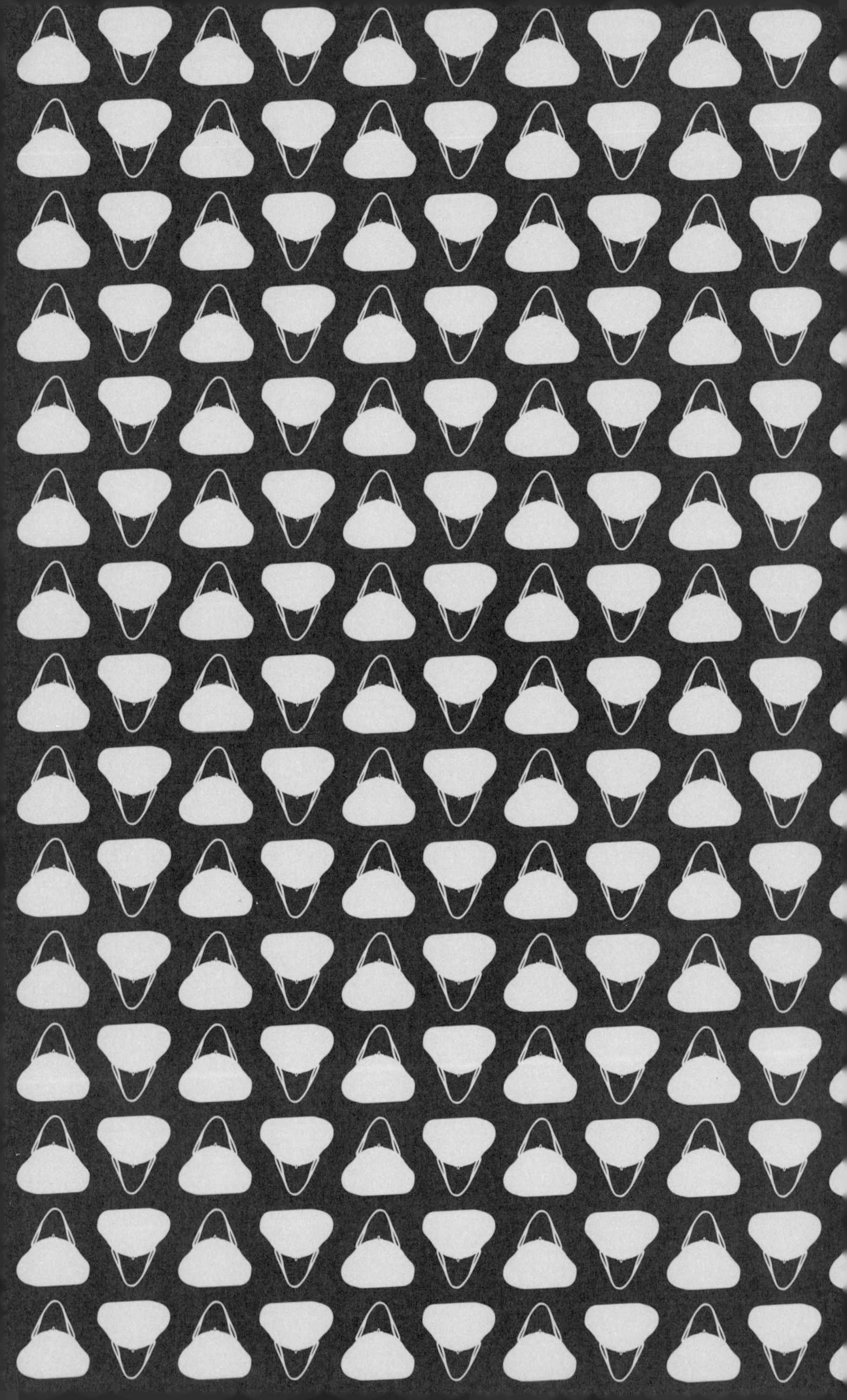